To Colin,
The dream is free.
The hustle is sold
seperately.

Black Licorice

A NOVEL BY

Camille Creates

Camille Creates

www.camillecreatesllc.com

ISBN: 978-1-09838-021-2

Copyright 2021 by Camille Creates

Written by: Camille Creates for Camille Creates LLC

Book edits: BookBaby Publishing

Manufactured by: BookBaby Publishing

Text formation: BookBaby Publishing

Cover sketch design: Garfield Dawkins

Cover graphics design: Jhade Gales for Jhade Gales Designs

Photography: Noel Pettigrew for Primelens Photography

DEDICATION

This book is blessed by the memory of my mommy, Karen Delores.

You taught me how to pray, laugh, smile, and glow. I sing in the daylight and dance in the moonlight, enlightened by the faithful spirit of the Lord.

Thank you for guiding my heart towards God's love and grace.

Your fiery spirit and compassion are eternally in my heart and soul.

Rest my love in purpose and peace.

You are my first true love.

Chica, I love you!

"Blessed is she who has believed that the Lord would fulfill his promises to her."

Luke 1:45

This book is dedicated to my son, Charles Toussaint.

Your creative spirit, strong will, kind heart, and thirst for knowledge inspire me every day.

You are my #PrinceCharles, my forever love.

May your life be filled with an abundance of blessings, love, light, and truth.

Poppa, I love you!

CONTENTS

PREFACE

"Self-love Attracts True Love"

My life is not perfect – my life is PROGRESSIVE.

My life is not about trials and tribulations – my life is about TRANSFORMATION.

My life is not about lost relationships – my life is about ENGAGING CONNECTIONS.

My life is not about fear – my life is about FAITH.

My life is not about being – my life is about BECOMING.

Today, I ask the Lord to forgive my SINS.

Today, I thank the Lord for his FAVOR, FAMILY, and FRIENDS.

Today, I thank the Lord for his GUIDANCE and GRACE.

Today, I thank the Lord for shepherding my PURPOSE and PRAYER.

INTRODUCTION

"Please Allow Me to Introduce Myself"

Darling KiKi, 33
Story

I love to watch BET, Marvel, and DC Comics. I enjoy the film series of *Harry Potter, The Twilight Saga,* and *The Godfather.* I adore *Love Jones,* laugh hysterically at the *Madea* movies and get amp for *James Bond* movies.

I listen to Rhythm and Blues, Hip hop, and Contemporary music.

I am Fiery, Energetic, and Adventurous.

I like Yoga, Brunch, Beer, and Bourbon.

"Having hope will give you courage." Job 11:18

I work hard during the week so I can play hard on the weekends. I live for moments that stir your soul and shake your spirit. I believe there are no shortcuts in life, only shortcomings. I love visiting art galleries, international travel, and coffee.

#WestPhilly #GirlBoss #DopeGirl #BrunchBabe #GodsChild

Please allow me to introduce myself. My name is Nikita Simone Brown. My friends call me KiKi. K to the I to the K to the I. That's my online dating profile above. Yes, I'm single.

There are a multitude of dating sites. These dating sites use match-making algorithms to present the perfect match. You swipe right to find your potential partner. Generally, you are matched with someone who shares the same or similar interests: for instance, sports, travel, entertainment, and recreation. You can't navigate through these sites alone. Fortunately, I have my #girlsquad or #brunchbabes[1] as I affectionately like to call them - Joie, Brandy, Nicole, and RiRi. I am also blessed to have Ivy. Ivy is my inner voice. Ivy is like my co-pilot. She makes sure I'm traveling in the right lane and paying attention to the traffic lights. I know - Red means STOP, Yellow means SLOW DOWN, and Green means GO, but sometimes Ivy has to remind me. Ivy and my brunch babes work in tandem together like a traffic app – they find the best route and redirect me away from detours.

In my twenties, dating was easy, effortless, and fun. In my thirties, the lines are blurred between a casual friend with benefits, emotional intimacy, or a commitment connection. If you have ever tried online dating, then you know it is a tedious process. First, you craft a profile – highlighting the best version of yourself. Ugh! In some cases, I have seen a fairy-tale profile that ended up being a horror story. Second, you need a profile pic. Be careful – you don't want to seem too thirsty or desperate. My girls and I have shot hundreds of photos to find the best lighting, angles, and presence. Whew! Finally, a pic I like – my smile is perfect and the light captures my dopeness. Third, you have to decide which online dating site matches your mood and temperament.

I stumbled across an online dating site that guaranteed the best astro-logical matches. I'm a fire sign, Sagittarius! My first match was a fellow fire sign, Aries. The sex was explosive but the relationship bombed. My second

---

1   **Brunch Babes**, noun, A group of good, good girlfriends who enjoy bottomless Mimosas, French Toast, and Gossip.

profile match was plagued by the charisma of an Aquarius. He had a whole family – a wife and two kids. One day, we met for lunch and in the rear of his car was a child's booster seat. He attempted a story about his cousin borrowing his car. "Pull over. Pull over." Ivy yelled. I hit the brake hard at that red light. I should have swiped left instead of right for my next match with a Leo. Never expect for a Leo to put your needs before their own. He needed his ego stroked all the time. Ivy quoted Lil' Kim's *"Not Tonight."* "I give you ten G's, (expletive), if ya leave me alone."

A top pick match resulted in a fearless Aries. I swiped right to meet a sweet, intellectual and occasional quick-witted man. He was a great conversationalist and had a unique way of applying information in unconventional ways. We could talk about anything. Music and arts became our center. Ironically, we were good until we weren't. I slowed down at the yellow light. To this day, we are still good friends. Brandy liked him and Nicole always gave him a hard time.

I dated a Taurus and we were good, good. He was generous with a kind heart, and a stubborn streak. He never played follow the leader. His faith created within him, a spirit of determination which propelled his steadfast knack for creating business ventures. Time and space separated us, but we always had this kinetic energy holding us together no matter where in the world either us resided. In that relationship, I learned with love and patience nothing is impossible.

Dating reminds me of summers on Vine Street, playing "1-2-3, Red Light, Green Light." In the meantime, I am leaning into myself. I am staring back at my reflection in the mirror. Self-reflection forces me to examine and assess past relationships – personal and professional. Though my voyage of self-discovery, my past relationship with self has always been to keep my soul happy. I keep negative people and thoughts at bay. I love my family and friends. I work hard and remain humble but, most importantly, I love ME. Honesty is my truth and I am unapologetic for its delivery. It's my story. I can rewrite the next chapter.

God and I talk all the time. I don't always pray for something. Most times I pray a thankful prayer. As I hike through the dating jungle, my compass is my KiKi prayer. You know ... like the CiCi prayer – Russell Wilson and Ciara! See, you know her prayer. My mother always reminds me, be specific when you posture for prayer. Prayer is powerful and requires patience. God has a bigger plan for you than you have for yourself. Wait on the Lord. God's timing is perfect!

By the way, my mother's name is Delores. Delores is a retired insurance arbitrator. My dad's name is Jesse. Jesse recently retired after forty years of owning and operating a parking garage. I am their only child.

I listen attentively to my inner voice, Ivy. Ivy delivers mental, physical, and spiritual nutrients to me. Ivy says what she wants when she wants. Ivy is in large my spiritual mentor and coach. She is my good, good girlfriend. Did you know the ivy plant can grow in the hardest conditions? It grows in the direction of the sun. Ivy represents dependence and attachment, which can be seen in the way it climbs buildings. It also symbolizes love and friendship.

Well, enough about me and more about my journey. The best way to tell a story is to start at the beginning. Please prepare for my genesis.

CHAPTER 1 –

"The 'Z' Lounge"

The Philly Jawn Magazine calls the "Z" Lounge a premier destination for vibrant and alluring fun. Step inside a globally inspired dance party mixed with seductive drink menus and sultry music. First Saturday at the "Z" is described as carnival in Philly.

Our squad goal is to have a night of flirtatious fun at the "Z" Lounge. The reviews are five-star and the cocktail selections are hangover worthy. We all agree to "Girls Night" on first Saturday. My appointment for my hair and nails is confirmed. Pregame is at eight.

Except for networking events, it has been ages since I've been out. Selecting the perfect outfit is an arduous task. I have everything to wear but nothing to wear. I commit to wearing my palazzo pants and halter top. I grab a waist chain and a pair of gold post earrings. I style my locs up in a bun and color my lips red.

"Ok Suga, you're going to make somebody cuckoo for cocoa puffs." Ivy compliments.

When we arrive at the club, the line is stretched down 2nd Street. We quickly advance to the front of the line. Inside we are greeted by a laser light show. The magical effects of the strobe lights play against the rhythm of the DJ's spin. The music ripples through a state-of-the-art sound system. DJ Tra has full command of the thundering crowd. The ambiance is lush, sultry, and saucy.

The "Z" Lounge located in the Piazza of Northern Liberties boasts two dance floors, three bars, and two VIP lounges. Designed in a Moroccan fili-gree scroll are brass dividers that can be moved to create a large VIP area. The VIP areas are lit in glowing purple and gold. There is a full bottle service, a rooftop deck, and a cigar bar. "Z" has a sunken lounge pit with plush navy velvet-tufted seating. The Lucite table in the center blushes in pink. Lining the bars are acrylic drink menus backlit in a gold hue. The ambiance is royal with its plush velvet jewel-tone hues and tufted sofas in amethyst, emerald green, marigold, and navy. Resting atop the club sits an office with a glass orb design.

I look up to catch a glimpse of an inky, dark shadow. Wow! From up there you have a whole view of the club. We find a section close to the dance floor, easy access to the bar, and most importantly, the bathroom. The bottle girls are dressed in "brnd.n3w".[2] The "Z" girls are insanely busy - glasses are clinking and bottles are clanking. Somehow, I miss my cue to order a drink. Everyone is sippin' so I strut towards the bar.

"Hi! May I have a Manhattan with Maker's Mark? Please!"

The moment I order my drink, God turns water into wine. Tall, hand-some, dark, salacious, sweet, and spicy – like a piece of black licorice. *"Yaaasss!"* This foiinneee man is standing to the right of me. His crown is topped with a taper fade and 180 waves. *"Oooh!"* He is a member of the Philly Beard Gang. I admire his style. He is casually dressed in a navy-blue suit, a crisp white shirt, and a pair of blue Adidas Superstars.

"Girl, he doesn't have a ring on." Ivy notes.

"Hi, are you enjoying yourself?" asks a soft but masculine voice.

I turn and answer with a huge smile. "Hi, I am actually. This is my first time here. How about you – are you enjoying yourself?"

---

2   **brnd.n3w**, noun, Casual clothing of style worn especially by members who don't follow trends but inspire them.

"I am actually having a great time now. My name is Elijah and you are?"

"Nikita!" I return.

I extend my arm to shake his hand. "It is a pleasure to meet you, Elijah!"

"You have a firm handshake." Elijah states.

"Thank you!" I reply.

The bartender interrupts, "Boss, can I get you anything?"

"No, thank you. Yvonne, I'm good." Elijah replies.

"Oh, my apologies, Mr. Elijah." I snicker.

"Part of my job is to ensure my patrons are enjoying themselves." Elijah explains.

"Well, Mr. Elijah, it is early in the evening to say for sure. But my girls and I are poised to have fun tonight. I should let you get back to work and mingle with your other guests?"

"You are the only guest I want to talk to."

"Well, you are the boss!" I declare.

"Time for some action." Ivy directs.

"Mr. Elijah, what do your friends call you?" **"E, bruh, or dawg."**

"What does your mother call you?" **"Eli."**

"What do your children call you?" **"My daughter calls me, Dada."**

"What does your daughter's mother call you?" **"Asshole."**

My curiosity peaks and I laugh.

"You have a cute laugh." Elijah notes.

Shaking my head, "I'm sorry. I didn't mean to laugh. Honestly. Yes, I did!"

Elijah chuckles along with me. His full beard, lips, and teeth are perfect. He is perfect!

"So Nikita, what do your friends call you?" **"KiKi."**

"What does your mother call you?" **"Nikita or if she's mad at me, Nikita Simone."**

"What do your children call you?" **"I don't have any children."**

"What does your boyfriend call you?" **"His Ex."**

Elijah's eyes widen as he smiles.

"What should I call you?" I ask.

"Baby." Elijah asserts.

"Now Mr. Elijah, that warrants excellent customer service!"

"Nikita, you should take full advantage of our rewards program." Elijah insists.

"Sounds intriguing. Maybe later you can explain the program in further detail. I better get back to my girls before they worry I'm lost."

"Hopefully, we can continue this discussion later." Elijah contends.

Curiosity gleams in his eyes. "What should I call you?" Elijah asks.

I grab my drink and move in really close to Elijah. "Darling KiKi," I purr in his ear. I sass back to the lounge. Elijah's spicy sweet smell lingers. I turn around to find him still taking note of me. At some point during our exchange, Yvonne pours him a drink – something brown. I am blushing to learn more about his rewards program. Back over in the lounge pit, Joie, Brandy, Nicole, and RiRi have made themselves comfortable.

"This sofa is so comfortable. I'm about to take a nap." Nicole says.

"I am about to get my life on the dance floor. The DJ is jammin'." Joie laughs.

"I'm good right here. I can see any and everything." RiRi notes.

"Wait! Where is KiKi?" Brandy asks.

"She took her hot ass to get a drink." Joie replies.

"Where the hell was she when we ordered?" Nicole blurts.

"Here comes the Quitch[3] now. Where the hell have you been?" RiRi yells.

"I was at the bar! I was talking with the owner." I present.

"Damn Quitch! You are always in work mode." Joie quips.

"I'm done." Nicole laughs.

"Deets." Brandy begs.

"Spicy! Handsome! Sweet! His smell is so delicious! Gurlll! He's in the beard gang! Look, he is over my shoulder at the bar wearing a dark colored suit."

"What's his name?" Nicole quizzes.

"Elijah!"

"Gurlll, he is fine." RiRi adds.

"Right!"   ·

"He is a jawn!"[4] Brandy compliments.

"He is looking over here. Girl, what did you say to him?" Nicole probes.

"Small talk. He's single – I think. He has a little girl."

"His eyes are still fixated on you. You go girl!" Brandy inspires.

DJ Tra got the whole club jumpin'. It feels like carnival on the dance floor – sexy and hot. I am feelin' myself or maybe it's the Manhattans that are feelin' all over me. I sure wish Mr. Elijah was feelin' all over me.

Wishes do come true. Elijah's touch is around my waist. His honeyed breath is on my neck. Elijah's rhythm matches my rhythm against Rotimi's *"Love Riddim"*. "Hi Darling KiKi," he whispers in my ear. "I told you I would come looking for you." I feel a flutter in my stomach, a tingle in my vajayjay, and a loud drum beat my heart. "Oooh Baby." Ivy moans.

---

3   **Quitch**, noun, A "Queen Bitch" who has the tendency to display a resting bitch face and/or behavior.

4   **Jawn**, noun, (Philly dialect) used to refer to a thing, place, person, or event that one need not or cannot give a specific name to.

In Philly, you can always time the last call for alcohol when the DJ plays *"Maniac"* by Eve.

"Take a walk with me. Let's get some air." Elijah insists.

Elijah takes hold of my hand and leads the way to the rear of the club. He inserts his key in the elevator and presses a button. We enter the elevator and seconds later, the doors open to a sprawling rooftop deck. The air is brisk and the black sky above sparkles.

"Is this part of the rewards program?" I joke.

Elijah slopes in and kisses me. His tongue is long and determined. His redolence is intoxicating. Elijah's grip is strong and assertive but caressing and careful. There are African drums beating. The moment reached a musical climax – like in the movies. Damn, it's my phone ringing.

"Girl, where are you? The club is closing." Nicole yells.

"Oh my! I'm coming. I stepped out for some air."

"Stepped out where?" Nicole inquires.

"Here I come." I respond.

"Elijah, I have to go. My girls are looking for me."

"Have breakfast with me."

"Breakfast?" I ask.

"Yes!" Elijah exclaims.

I bite my lip pondering his request. "I'll have breakfast with you." I accede. "But can we order coffee first?"

We both smile and head to the elevator. Back in the club, my girls are waiting at the bar.

"Girl, they gon' kick us out of here." Joie blurts.

"No they won't. Let me introduce you all to Elijah. Elijah owns "Z." We were just discussing the highlights of his loyalty rewards program."

"Hell! No one provided us that level of customer service." Nicole jeers.

Elijah laughs, "I will coach my staff to serve you better next time."

"Would you all like to join Nikita and me for breakfast?"

"Breakfast?" Joie quips.

"Thank you. We are all pretty tired." Brandy announces.

"I want to take these damn shoes off." Nicole hisses.

Elijah turns to me. "Undoubtedly, we are hungry. I will deliver you home safely." Elijah promises.

RiRi cuts Elijah an evil eye. "You betta." She cautions.

"What is your last name? You might be a ring-leader in a sex trafficking plot." Nicole presses.

"Alexander. Elijah Alexander." He offers.

I kiss my girls. "Be careful driving and please get home safely."

"You get home safely." RiRi demands.

Elijah asks me to wait at the bar while he reconciles the numbers from this evening.

"Yvonne, can you please make Nikita a cup of coffee?" Elijah manners. "I won't be long."

He winks his eye and strolls to the elevator. Yvonne makes me an espresso. The vision from the rooftop frolics in my head, I smile and sip. Yvonne is cleaning the bar area and counting her register. Yvonne is intrigued by the novelty of Elijah's behavior. Yvonne turns her attention over to me.

"Nikita! Right? What did you do to my boss? Elijah rarely hangs in the lounge. I have never seen him on the dance floor. Elijah only frequents the lounge area to commingle with celebrities or VIP. You must be a VIP."

"I don't know. Elijah just appeared as I was ordering my drink." I blush.

Elijah emerges about twenty minutes later. "What are you two chatting about?"

Yvonne and I turn to each other and break out into a girlish laughter.

"You!" We both pant in unison.

"Yvonne, you are not sharing insider secrets are you?"

"Absolutely not!" Yvonne giggles.

"Yvonne, thank you for a smooth night. Tonight's numbers for the bar are exceptional."

They high-five each other. "Thank you, Boss. It was - lit tonight. Nikita, it was nice to meet you!"

"Yvonne, nice to meet you too. Thank you for the coffee. Your coffee is as good as your Manhattans."

I tip Yvonne again. Yvonne grins and salutes us goodbye. Elijah bids good night to the rest of his team. "Thank you for a great night."

I walk with Elijah to the elevator. We descend to the garage. Elijah clicks his key fob and the lights glare on a shiny black Range Rover. Elijah opens my door. What appears to be his signature fragrance permeates the Range. As I settle in the passenger seat, he positions his hand between my legs.

"Darling KiKi, what do you have a taste for?" Elijah whispers.

"Mr. Elijah, what do you have a taste for?" I tease.

Winking and pecking my lip, "You!"

"Where are you taking me?" I prod.

"I know a quaint spot with the best bacon and eggs. Are you still down?"

"Yes, I am hungry." I respond.

In the same impressionistic display as from the rooftop, the stars twinkle through the sunroof; the night air is cool and crisp. We pull into a loft space on Columbia Avenue in Fishtown. Elijah exits the Range, walks to my side, and opens my door. Elijah grabs my hand, leading the way towards an elevator. Inside the elevator, Elijah rests his muscular body against mine, his tongue slithers along my lips. The elevator halts and opens up to a massive loft.

The interior is modern industrial – masculine and clean. The loft is wrapped in a palette of black and gray with subtle hints of ivory. The styling has a Restoration Hardware vibe. The windows framed in black iron are expansive, exposed concrete and iron-clad beams hang above. The walls are painted African Gray and are set off by Cashmere Gray oak floors in a chevron pattern. Aligning the wall is a portrait of "Questlove" by painter Kehinde Wiley. There is also a painting called the "The Harem Guard" by Jean Discart.

In the living room sits a camel-colored leather sectional covered with mud cloth pillows. The coffee table has an organic appeal in the way the veins of black marble flow into white marble. The elements of yin and of yang balance the energy in the room. Atop the coffee table are purple agate coasters and a gray marble bowl with clear quartz crystals. The martini side tables have a gray cement base.

The shelves in the study are sprawling with books by Ralph Ellison, Michael Eric Dyson, Nathan McCall, and Elijah Muhammad. There are autobiographies of Michelle and Barack Obama, Malcolm X, Frederick Douglass, and Che Guevara. He has the *"Rich Dad, Poor Dad"* series and several books by Robert Green including *"Seduction."* Other titles include, *"The Millionaire Next Door," "The Monk Who Sold His Ferrari," "The Alchemist,"* and *"The Intelligent Investor."* Adorning one of the shelves is an Omega Psi Phi shield and paddle. A crest pin sits in a velvet silk-lined box. In the middle of the study sits a black marble pool table with gray felt and custom pool balls.

"Welcome to Cafe de Eli!" Elijah announces.

Elijah removes his blazer. He gestures for my clutch, placing it upon a stool. Elijah accompanies me down the hall to the bathroom. He adorned the bathroom with purple "Harlem Toile de Jouy."

"You can freshen up in here." Elijah suggests.

"Thank you!" I offer.

"Cafe de Eli! Seriously? We are not eating breakfast at a diner – in a public place. What am I doing at this fine ass man's loft?" I ponder in the mirror.

I text my girls his license plate number and quick details about the loft. I will have to deal with the "Are you crazy?" rhetoric later.

"Nikita, what are you doing here? Girl sex trafficking is real." Ivy counsels.

I unite with Elijah in the kitchen where a rich aroma of maple makes me salivate. Alongside him is an older woman.

"Nikita, this is Ms. Vela – Ms. Carla Vela. Ms. Vela is my house manager. Ms. Vela also helps me care for my daughter, Zoe."

"Hi Ms. Vela. It is a pleasure to meet you!"

"Hello Nikita, the pleasure is mine. I hope you enjoy the breakfast."

"Thank you. I'm sure I will. It smells delish."

"Elijah, will there be anything else?"

"No, thank you, Ms. Vela. Thank you for preparing this meal at such short notice."

"No worries. I was already in the kitchen prepping the dinner for tomorrow. Well then if there is nothing else, I will leave you two alone. Good night!" Ms. Vela retires down the hall to her bedroom.

On the counter is a pot of fresh brewed coffee and bacon and egg sandwiches on ciabatta bread. This is either the best sandwich eva' eva' or I needed to cross the Manhattan Bridge of cocktails. The Spanish coffee is delicioso.

"What is your review of Cafe de Eli?" Elijah asks.

"I rate it a Perfect 10! What's your average rating?" I investigate.

Elijah's jet black, thick eyebrows arch.

"How many other guests have you enrolled in the loyalty rewards program?" I continue.

"You're my first loyalty member," Elijah cleverly responds.

Hard to believe ... because this man is fine and flavorsome. Oh, did I mention foiinneee?

"Nikita, I spotted you the moment you set your pretty self in my club. Your smile, confidence, and sexy strut caught my attention immediately. I couldn't wait for the perfect moment to talk to you. I followed you to the bar."

"Wow! I appreciate the compliment."

After eating, we move to the living room sofa. The time morphs into hours of conversation and laughter. We chat about our family, friends, past relationships, and work. Elijah's owned and operated the "Z" Lounge for a little over four years. He also manages a real estate investment portfolio. I share with him that I am a commercial banker. Of course, I suggest he let me review his bank relationship.

"Okay! Sexy and smart!" Elijah quips.

Elijah's daughter, Zoe, is three years old. The relationship with Barbara, Zoe's mother, was short-lived. The relationship ended before Zoe's first birthday. As for me, the night comes to a tiring end. Elijah covers me with a feather-gray faux-fur blanket. He slumbers as well – falling asleep at the opposite end of the sofa.

I awake a few hours later. Elijah's dark-chocolate skin melts into the camel-colored sofa. I transfer my blanket to Elijah and escape outside onto the balcony. The sky brightens with an apricot-orange sunrise. The air is cool, breezy. I sneeze several times. Elijah wakes and steps out onto the balcony – blanket in hand. He drapes us both. Elijah's broad shoulders and chiseled chest are jacked underneath a white tank. His pants hang lazy minus his belt.

"I'm sorry. I didn't want to wake you," I whisper.

Elijah's silence is seductive. As the sun rises and glows upon the sky, Elijah twirls me around facing him. His tongue possessing my mouth and throat. Elijah sweeps me up around his waist. His kiss accompanies our journey down the hall to his master bedroom. Gently kissing along my neck and shoulders, tugging off my clothes. Elijah's lips are wet and warm. His teeth biting at my ears. His sensual lips kiss my neck, shoulders, breasts, and stomach. Elijah slips off my panties. His lips and tongue travel where my forbidden fruit lies. Elijah's tongue is sinful; the pleasure is concentrated and intense.

His soft, strapping hands caress my hips. My moan is unhurried and steady. My legs lock around his neck. My clit tingles like peppermint. My insides tickle like a feather. From my core, juice spills like lava. The velocity of the flow pours into an eruption. I cover my scream with his pillow. He gets up to secure a condom – removing his pants and briefs. Elijah enters my body with a deep plunge and deliberate strokes. Rapping in my head is Meek Mill and Rick Ross, *"I'm a Boss."*

"Gurlll. Mr. Elijah is a boss in bed." Ivy moans.

I wake to what I believe is a dream. The satisfying savor in the sheets and the sound of the shower quickly remind me of the night before and the present. Elijah's bedroom transports you to Bali. A king-size bed centers the room. The linen headboard is covered in a rich hue of gold; the texture is soft to the touch. His night stands are hexagonal antique brass. The flooring in the living room runs throughout the entire loft. A Turkish pendant light hung above casts a glow of shadows on the ceiling. A sheepskin rug fleeces warmth under your feet.

I jump from the bed and enter the master bathroom. The steam rises out from the shower. Elijah turns and shines a devilish grin through the glass door. On his muscular back is a large tattoo of a phoenix blazing through fire and ash. I step into the shower grabbing onto his arm branded with a Greek symbol, $\Omega\Psi\Phi$. My arms cross under his – lathering soap from the peak of his ripped torso, down the curve of his pelvis, around the shred of his back. Elijah turns and tattooed on his chest is the name "Zoe" in cursive with a crown on top. Elijah spins my hips around and places my hands up on the shower tiles. He grabs a condom near the soap dish. Did he anticipate I would desire more? He clutches my ass cheeks, penetrating me from behind. My moan is heavy against the rock climb of his penis. Elijah asserts his thrusts, dominating every stroke. Elijah grazes the back of my neck. The span of his strokes lessens; he grabs tight at my waist and releases a heavy moan. Elijah's breathing hurries as he leans hard against my ass.

"Are you okay?" Elijah whispers.

"Yes." I purr.

Elijah foams a washcloth, gently brushing against my legs, tush, and my pretty pudenda. Elijah gets dressed quick and heads to the kitchen. I trail behind his shadow, dressed in yesterday's clothes, locs dangling. During the day, sunlight floods the loft with energy. A yogi would find perfect form here.

Elijah rises from the counter, twirling my locs through his fingers. "Nice! A little lion queen."

An enormous smile radiates across my face.

"Are you hungry?" He asks.

"No, thank you. I would love some coffee."

"Are you in a hurry to get home?"

"I'm in no rush. I do want to change out of these clothes."

"You should call your girlfriends and let them know you're safe."

"You think." I joke.

Elijah's brow lifts, and his chuckle is playful and warm.

"Where is Ms. Vela?"

"Ms. Vela has off on Sundays and Mondays."

"What are your plans for the day?" I inquire.

"I have Zoe today. She lives here with Ms. Vela and me Sunday through Wednesday. Zoe has a tea party planned for us today." Elijah grins.

Elijah and I picked up our discussion right where we left off this morning. The sun dims its glow midway through the day when Elijah pulls in front of my house. There is no place like home, yet this moment feels bittersweet as I gaze upon Elijah. Elijah removes his seat belt, exits the car, and circles around to open my door.

"When will I get to see you again?" Elijah hints.

"My work schedule is flexible. My evenings are free, unless I have to attend a networking event."

"Can I take you to dinner on Tuesday? Ms. Vela returns then."

"Absolutely!" I blurt. "Elijah, I had a wonderful time."

"I had a great time too, Nikita."

We kiss hard, then taper to soft pecks. His piquant scent carries me up the steps. I spin to tender him goodbye and his smile tickles at my clit. He beeps the horn and the Range peels off.

"Oh, what a night!" I exhale.

Not long after I change into something comfortable, the doorbell rings. He's back!

"Is it Tuesday already?" I joke.

"Lol! You forgot something." Elijah quips.

"Are you sure? I checked. I have all of my belongings."

"We forgot to exchange numbers. It wasn't my intent for this to be a one-night stand.

You can't get rid of me that easily."

"I left my business card on your night stand." I note.

"Great, but I'm here now. You can put your number in my phone. You look cute and comfortable."

He kisses me on my cheek and skips down the steps. Elijah joins a Face-Time call, "Where are you, Dada?"

I send a group text to my girls, "I'm home, safe and sound." I kick back on the sofa and replay the night in my head. *Did last night actually happen? Who is this man? Why is he single? Forgive me, Lord. I gave it up on the first night. Regrets? Nope!*

Later in the evening, I settle in to watch *The ReidOut*. The fragrant spice of Elijah whiffs under my nose. The visions from this morning dance like fairies in my head. A surge of heat presses between my legs. I feel a vibration near my side. Oh my! It's my phone. Excited, I answer a FaceTime call from Elijah.

"Hey, Nikita!"

"Hi, Elijah!"

"Is this a good time for you talk?" He asks.

"Sure. I am lounging in front of the television. What about you?"

"Thinking about you!" Elijah admits.

As I ready myself to ask, "Where is your daughter?" I hear the purity and playfulness in the innocence of a young girl's voice.

"Dada, who you talking to?"

"My friend, Ms. Nikita."

"Your friend is a girl?" Zoe queries.

"Yes, Zoe."

"Dada, you have a girlfriend?"

"Ms. Nikita is a friend who happens to be a girl."

An adorable, little girl with brown sugar deep dimples and two round Afro puffs peeks her face and giggles into the phone.

"Hello, Miss Zoe. You are an adorable little princess!"

Zoe giggles, "Dada, she called me a princess!"

"You are a princess. Daddy's princess!" Elijah responds.

Zoe giggles gleefully, hugging Elijah.

"Is your friend a princess?"

"No, Ms. Nikita is a queen."

"Dada, what are you?"

"Zoe, your father is a king."

"Dada, you're a king?

"If Ms. Nikita says so, I'm a king!"

Zoe yawns and crawls over to the side of the bed. Not long after, Zoe is fast asleep.

"The tea party must have been fun."

"Zoe wore herself out jumping and running through the loft."

"Elijah, you must be pretty tired yourself."

"I am, but your perfume in my bed is tantalizing. It's keeping me alert."

"Honestly, I had an amazing time with you."

"I did too." Elijah confesses. "I'm not sure I can wait until Tuesday to see you again."

"I don't get into the city much on Mondays; I work from home. On Mondays, I am completely inundated with conference calls and admin work."

"The same for me. Generally on Mondays, Yvonne and I place supply and liquor orders for the club. I also coordinate general contracting schedules for my properties. I currently have two investment properties in the inspection phase."

"Where are the properties located?" I inquire.

"The 900 block of North 45th street."

"Mill Creek!"

"Yes! You know your city."

"I should. I was born and raised here." I note.

"What do you do for fun?" Elijah asks.

"What every woman does. Shop! I also love art galleries, wine tastings, antique shops, and shopping for home decor and international coffee."

"Coffee! Really? I can't tell it." Elijah laughs.

"I love the art collection in your loft." I compliment.

"Thank you! I know nothing about art. I buy what speaks to me." Elijah concedes.

"Art collecting is about what speaks to you, what speaks to your soul." I proclaim. "Art appeals to everyone differently. Art challenges your eye to what feels special to you."

"Like when I saw you in the club - your smile spoke and my soul listened." Elijah claims.

"Surely?" I smirk.

"Yes! Your smile lights up a room. Catching a glimpse of you from my office lit up the whole club."

"Is the glass arch part of your office?"

"Yes!"

"Cool! That was your shadow I saw Saturday night. I love the design elements, the jewel tones regale the space. The color hues are noble against the plush texture and the Lucite materials. The arch details, the look of Middle Eastern grandeur. I imagine there is a worldly view from up there."

"I'll give you a private tour. I designed the space with a passionate designer, Elaine Darien. Elaine listened carefully and captured every detail in the plans. I was envisioning 'Arabian Nights' and she completely brought it to life."

"What motivated you to open a nightclub?" I ask.

"There wasn't anything grown and sexy in the city. I wanted the allure of a high-end lounge with excitement and safe fun. Operating the club takes a lot of my time and attention, but I really enjoy it."

"How did you come to invest in real estate?" I probe.

"I established a real estate portfolio to create generational wealth for Zoe. The gentrification in the city intrigued me. Areas like Northern Liberties and Fishtown, once industrial and plagued with addicts, now have an urban community vibe. A few of my fraternity brothers and I partner in the real estate investment projects. We are on a mission to revitalize parts of Philly that were once thriving black communities. We also manage and superintend our own properties."

"You are doing well for yourself and Zoe."

"I'm trying. I'm not done. I need a queen to share it with."

"Zoe will be a queen someday."

"I know, but I need a queen to build with now."

I smile, "Well, you better get on your job then."

Elijah fights back a yawn. "Elijah, you should get some rest. We can talk again tomorrow."

"Agreed. Sweet dreams."

I blow him a kiss, "I hope you find your queen in your dreams."

"That's easy. You are my dream."

CHAPTER 2 –
"Tom Ford"

I toss and turn all through Sunday night, not getting much sleep. I was not able or willing to get the moments with Elijah out of my head. Monday was absent in its normal rapid pace. Around 1:00 p.m., I receive a text from Elijah with a *sleeping face, cloud,* and *crown* emoji. I text back an *aww* and *kissy face* emoji. I was in a trance when the blaring ring of the doorbell startled me. "I have a delivery for Ms. Brown." I sign for a huge white box. Contained in the white box are twenty-four bright, fiery orange roses and a note. The note reads: "'I hope these roses make you blush ... the way I blush when I think of you.' Your future king, Elijah!"

"Oh my!" I pinch myself. I swear I am going to wake up from a dream soon. I hurry to dial Elijah's number. A delighted but strapping voice answers on the other end of the line.

"Nikita! Hi!"

"Hi, Elijah!"

"How is your day?" He asks.

"It is pacing like a snail. Although, brightened when I received your beautiful flowers. Thank you! I am blushing!"

"You're welcome!"

"Elijah, what about you? How is your day?"

"My day is great! I have a whole movie playing in my head." Elijah shares.

"What is the name of the movie?" "Seduction?" I query.

"Nikita, whatever do you mean?" Elijah jesters.

"Are the flowers a peace offering for seducing me this past weekend?"

"Now Nikita! I thought that is what 'Darling KiKi' wanted." Elijah replies with unrestrained laughter.

"Touche, Mr. Elijah!"

"Ha-ha!" We both chuckle.

I can hear someone in the background yelling, "Bruh."

"Elijah, I wanted to call and thank you for the flowers."

"I'm glad you called."

"We should probably both get back to working." I hint.

"I agree."

A couple of seconds later Elijah calls back.

"Hello."

"I am on my job. You are going to be my queen." Elijah discloses.

Elijah and I didn't talk on the phone Monday night. I become one with my bed and I bet Elijah and Zoe did the same.

I welcome Tuesday with pure excitement. I am elated about having dinner with Elijah tonight. My phone rings in the dawn of a new day.

"Hello."

I'm greeted by Elijah, "Good morning, Nikita! Did I wake you?"

"No. Good morning!"

"Did you sleep well?" Elijah asks.

"I slept very well. Thank you."

"Zoe and I crashed early last night."

"I did too."

"What do you have on?" Elijah queries.

"A silk nightgown."

My attention is diverted when the doorbell rings. Curious, I reach for my robe and ask Elijah to please hold on. *Who in the hell is at my door this early?* I wonder. I peek through the window and to my surprise – it is Elijah! My heart races. His allure is deliciously fascinating – even in sweats. I disarm the alarm and pull open the door.

"Good morning, Baby girl! I hope I'm not intruding. I brought breakfast."

"No, not at all. Please come in."

"Surprised?" He asks.

Elijah places his hand around my waist and kisses me. "Again, I hope I'm not invading your space. I couldn't wait until tonight to see you."

"This is a welcome surprise! You must be an early riser. Where is Zoe?"

"I try for an early start before Zoe wakes up. Zoe is at home with Ms. Vela."

Elijah hands me a bag and a cup of coffee. "Here, I brought pancakes."

"Thank you! Please have a seat." I offer.

Elijah sits at the kitchen counter. He pulls me close – in between his legs.

"Can I see your nightgown?"

"I had to grab my robe to answer the door."

"Good thinking. You shouldn't be giving everyone on the block a peep show."

"Lol." I smirk.

"Nikita, let me set the record straight right now. You are going to be my right hand. From here on out, I'm not letting you out of my sight. This is the beginning. The beginning of us!"

This is a first for me, I am immobilized and speechless. This perfect, smart, determined, focused specimen is claiming me – claiming us.

"Girl, is Elijah a glow-up or a fuck-up?" Ivy presses.

Elijah slips my robe off my shoulders. I kiss him with fervent desire. I want him to know I vehemently agree with his decision. Mr. Elijah was officially campaigning to become my king!

"Girl, is Elijah a benevolent king or a dictator king? Inquiring minds want to know." Ivy cautions.

Elijah snatches at my waist. "Where is your bedroom?"

Elijah and I spoon in bed. His grin glows gorgeous in the sunlight. Suffice it to say, Elijah is a "G" in bed. Elijah tilts his head down to kiss my forehead.

"Thank God you chose to party at "Z" Saturday night."

Burying my head in his chest, "What kind of cologne do you wear?" I ask.

"Tom Ford Noir." Elijah answers.

The chorus of Jay Z's *"Tom Ford"* raps in my head. Elijah always smells like black licorice – candied with a hint of spice. Elijah's phone rings. I get up to shower as Elijah answers the call.

Showered and dressed, Elijah and I reconvene back in the kitchen. "I love your house. It has a cozy free-spirit vibe. Not a wild hippy child but classic boho."

"Thank you. I do live my life colorfully! I thought you didn't know anything about art."

"I don't really. But I do know a little about design and yours is Bohemian."

"Do you want me to warm your pancakes?" I ask.

"No, thank you. I have to get home and get Zoe ready for school."

"No worries. Thank you for breakfast!"

Heading for the door, Elijah grips his keys and taps my ass. "I will pick you up at seven for dinner."

CHAPTER 3 –

"First Date"

Throughout the day, I'm caught up in a rapture, daydreaming about Elijah. Butterflies dance in my stomach. I feel like a schoolgirl with her first crush. "This is the beginning of us," he declared this morning. This past weekend is one for urban history books. Girl goes to a premier nightclub. Girl sleeps with the nightclub owner. Girl dates the nightclub owner. Yaaasss!

"You saucy little minx jawn!" Ivy yells.

Elijah said he would be here at seven. I have no clue what to wear. I settle on my "Kimberly Goldson" gold hoodie, a faux leather flared miniskirt and a pair of leopard flats. Elijah arrives at 7:00 p.m. sharp. I greet him at the door with a hug and a kiss.

"Are you ready to leave now or would you like a pre-dinner cocktail or a beer?"

"I wouldn't mind a shot of something brown. If we stay any longer, I'm going to play under your skirt."

Elijah takes a shot of honeyed whisky. I grab him a water, arm the alarm, and lock up the house. He opens the Range door for me. As he climbs in the driver's seat, his phone rings. "My apologies, I must answer this call." I give a quick nod of acknowledgement.

"Dada, did you give it to her?"

"Zoe, not yet."

"Otay. Don't forget. I wuv you, Dada!"

"Zoe, I love you too. Now be sure to listen to Ms. Vela."

"I will, Dada. Bye, Dada. Kiss Kiss, Dada."

"I'm sorry. That was Zoe."

"No need to apologize."

Elijah scoops my hand into his. "Are you hungry?"

"I am starving."

"Good. 'Cause it's 'Taco Tuesday!'" You look cute! I've been thinking about how I like your hair – up versus down. Up in a bun – your vibe is naughty schoolteacher. Your vibe with your locs down is sexy lion queen. Either way I'm turned on."

Tonight, I went with naughty school-teacher. We shall see how the night unfolds.

"I've been running around the city all day. I ate those pancakes this morning and I had a smoothie this afternoon. I am starving too." Elijah mentions.

"Elijah, how was the rest of your day?" I ask.

"It was great!"

"What made it great?"

"I got a lot accomplished. The best part, my musings were all about you." Elijah winks.

We pull into the valet of a Spanish restaurant on Chestnut Street. "'Taco Tuesday' here we come!" Elijah exclaims. Elijah exits and rounds the Range to open my door. He supports my hand to help me down. The valet gives him a ticket and takes his keys. Inside, the hostess confirms our reservation and promptly seats us.

"When did you make a reservation?" I ask.

"After I ordered your roses."

"The roses were absolutely beautiful! Thank you!" I exclaim.

"You're welcome!"

Elijah unfastens his blazer and transports it to the hook outside our booth. Styling as usual, Elijah is dressed in a tan suit, a crisp white shirt, and white shell toe Adidas. He must have a closet full of Adidas. Interestingly enough, I have several pairs of the Adidas Grand Court style.

"The food here is amazing. This is one of Zoe's favorite restaurants. Zoe suggested I bring you here. She cried because she wanted to come too. Oh shit!"

Elijah hands me a scroll from his jacket pocket. "This is for you. Zoe drew it." I unroll a picture of a king, queen, and a princess. "As fate would have it, Zoe thinks her king needs a queen too." Elijah beams.

"Aww! This is beautiful! Please tell Zoe, thank you. I will frame it for my office."

"Zoe is happy I am happy."

"Elijah, how do you know this is happiness you are feeling? It has only been three days."

"Three days, three weeks, three months, three years, three decades! What is time surely if you waste it? I have enjoyed every moment talking to you." Elijah answers.

"Elijah, you say that now. You haven't seen my other side."

"Baby, I have seen all your sides." Elijah snickers.

"Hi. I'm Rosa. Can I get you both started with something to drink?"

"Yes, please. I will have a Watermelon Margarita." I reply.

"Yes, thank you. I'll have a Corona." Elijah orders.

"Ok. I will be back with your drinks and to take your order."

"Elijah, what's Zoe's favorite dish here?"

Elijah scans the menu options. "The 'Taco Tuesday Casserole' is Zoe's fav." He replies.

The casserole dish is lined with tortillas and topped with ground beef, corn, cheddar cheese, tomatoes, and olives with a dollop of sour cream. Elijah orders a cilantro lime rice with grilled chicken. Salsa music plays in the background. The waitress brings us some chips and salsa. Elijah requests a side of guacamole. He is HANGRY! He devours the nachos and wastes no time when the entrees arrive.

The waitress brings another round of drinks. Elijah scoots out the booth to sit next to me. "I would like to toast to royalty, royalty, royalty." Elijah sings. He sips his beer and turns his face to kiss me. "Did you like the food?" He asks.

"The food was delicious, but the bacon and egg sandwich still holds first place."

He laughs. "Wait until you taste my cooking."

"Wait. You cook too?"

"I got skills!" He boasts.

Elijah slides out the booth and extends his hand. "Dance with me."

The rhythm of a Spanish guitar invites us to the dance floor. We cha-cha-cha and salsa through the syncopation of drums, maracas, congas, and bongos. Our dance routine is joined by hysterical laughter. Others join us and some watch from the sidelines. As the music settles, we return to our booth for fried ice cream. Elijah smears ice cream on my cheek. When he advances to lick it off, I spin and push a cherry in his mouth.

"Elijah is fun!" Ivy giggles.

The waitress returns. "Can I get you both anything else?"

Elijah looks at me and I shake my head, "No. Thank you."

"Thank you. We will take the check." Elijah responds.

I excuse myself and cha-cha-cha to the ladies room. Elijah satisfies the check and stands in wait outside the ladies bathroom.

"Nikita, I paid the check. Are you ready?"

"Yes. I am ready. Thank you for dinner!"

"You're welcome!"

The valet pulls the Range up in front of the restaurant. Elijah opens my door. He tips the valet and hops in.

"Elijah, that was fun!"

"It was fun!" Elijah exclaims.

Elijah opens the sunroof. "Are you down for what's next?"

"Lead the way!"

"Now, where the fuck is he taking us?" Ivy grinds.

Elijah drives not far from the restaurant to a delightful secluded park ground. A beguiling garden lies in wake – mature trees, sprawling ivy, luscious lavender, sweet pink peonies and honeyed alyssums. Elijah gets out and lifts the trunk. He packed Prosecco and strawberries in a cooler. Elijah returns and slides back in with two glasses of Prosecco topped with radiant red strawberries.

"What are we toasting to?"

"Us! I think we might be good together."

"Clink!" "Clink!"

Elijah turns the dial to a satellite radio station. Usher's *"Tell Me"* croons softly through the Bose speakers.

"Do you want another glass?"

"No, thank you."

Elijah motions for my glass. He returns them to the cooler in the trunk. He opens my door and helps me down from the Range. We stroll over to a ravine of water. The cascade is serene and peaceful. A crescent moon ushers in the night.

"Am I moving too fast?" Elijah asks. "My spirit is keen when it comes to enterprising moves. My spirit is telling me to move next to you. I've enjoyed spending time with you. I want to spend a lot more."

Elijah is as enterprising as he is ambitious. Solidified by his amorous advances, I am crushing all over this man. "I am comfortable with our pace. I already shared my cookies. We don't need to spoil the milk."

He laughs hysterically. "You did share your chocolate mints. I had three great play dates."

I give him a sly look, and he grabs my waist and draws me into his chest. "See it is meant to be." Elijah says.

We walk to sit on a nearby bench. Bewitched on his side, "How did you find this park?"

"I jog here some days."

"It is beautiful – quiet and secluded." I note.

"I notice you forgot something." Elijah alludes. "I could tell on the dance floor that you don't have any underwear on."

"Yes, I do." I smirk.

"Let me see."

Elijah slides his hands under my skirt and lures my hips. He slides my thong to the side and skims across my forbidden fruit. Elijah probes his fingers in my pussy. He extracts his fingers, licking them. I engage his shoulders under the swell of my lips and clit. Elijah hoists me around his waist. He carries me back over to the Range. Elijah opens the back door and sets me down on the back seat. I kick off my flats unbuckling his belt. Elijah is hard on top of me. He pulls a condom from his wallet. Darkness and light still above. Elijah slips off my black thong. His hard penis enchants my warm pussy. We kiss hard and sloppy. His honeyed fingers in my mouth. His penis wedges against my pussy. I wrap my legs around his waist and endeavor to keep my moans quiet. The moistness between my legs increases with his powered thrusts. Elijah strokes, strokes, and strokes. His penis lodges deeper and deeper.

"Elijah." I moan.

"Nikita." He returns.

A discharge is near for both of us. Elijah exhales a loud moan. I match his moan as my body shakes under his. The weight of his body falls hard against mine.

Ivy quips, "Damn! I didn't know a Range had this much room in the rear."

CHAPTER 4 –

"Blackout"

The weeks with Elijah quickly advance. We have morning conversations after his daily run. We have afternoon conversations during our lunch breaks and evening FaceTime connections when he gets a break at the club. Our face-to-face time is limited by the club's schedule and his co-parenting responsibilities. We have breakfast together some mornings after his workouts. We meet for lunch other days when our work schedules allow. We always share together time on Sundays before he leaves to pick up Zoe. Elijah returns Zoe to her mother on Thursday afternoons. Every week, Zoe cries uncontrollably when she separates from Elijah. During those times, I can hear moments of unhappiness in Elijah's voice.

Today, I entertain taking Elijah to lunch. The blocks on my calendar quickly postpone that thought. I have back-to-back scheduled client appointments. Since Thursday starts the week of operations at the club, in all likelihood, he is enthralled too. Like clockwork, my phone rings early Friday morning.

"Good morning, Nikita!"

"Good morning, Elijah!"

"I have an idea – meet me at the loft. I will have breakfast and coffee waiting for you. You can get ready for work here."

Thankfully, my first client appointment isn't until 9:30 a.m. I grab my things and head out the door. As promised, breakfast and coffee are ready. Ms. Vela made cheese eggs, home fries, turkey sausage, and grits.

"Elijah, if I gain extra pounds, it is entirely Ms. Vela's fault."

Time is ticking. I clear the dishes. Elijah's phone rings. I use this opportunity to start getting ready for work. I carry on down the hall to the master bathroom. I shower and dress. When I return to the living room, I discover Elijah is still engaged in his phone conversation. Elijah is dismayed when I appear in the living room fully clothed. Elijah tugs at the zipper on my skirt. He pouts with a sad puppy dog gaze. He terminates his call uniting with me on the sofa.

"I apologize. I was working to find a replacement for tonight. My in-house singer called out sick."

Sadly for me, his weekends are largely dedicated to the club's operation. Elijah is quick to notice the woeful look on my face.

"Nikita, is everything okay?"

I kiss him and respond, "Yes!" "Elijah, I have to leave for work."

"When am I going to see you again?" Elijah asks.

"Can we play it by ear? Your weekend will be in full swing at the club."

He lures me in to kiss. His hands engage my thighs.

"Elijah, I have to go or I'm going to be late for my client appointment."

I spring from the sofa and shoot to the elevator. I blow him a kiss as the doors close.

Elijah texts me at 1:00 p.m., "Call me when you get a break." That break didn't come until 3:30 p.m.

"Finally!" Elijah belts on the phone. "I thought you forgot about me."

"Hi, Elijah! My day has been crazed. Besides, I don't think I could forget about you if I tried. What are you doin'?"

"I was about to dig into a salad. Sound check is in about thirty minutes for tonight's set. Did you eat yet?"

"Come to think of it, I haven't had anything to eat since this morning."

"Are you done at work yet?"

"Yes."

"Come to the club. I'll order you some food. You can eat and listen to sound check with me."

"Sounds like a plan. I'm on my way."

The club is massive in the daylight. Elijah is seated in a booth in front of the stage. I catch his eye and he slides out of the booth.

"Hi, beautiful! Aww. You look tired."

"I am – tired and hungry."

"Come sit down. I have your food at the booth. I ordered you a jerk salmon salad. You made it just in time. Sound check starts in five minutes. It is not my in-house singer, but Bonita is pretty fierce."

Bonita is an Afro-Cuban singer. Her sound check is lit. "Z" has live entertainment on Thursday and Friday evenings from 8:00 p.m. until 9:30 p.m. The "Z" also has Happy Hour on Thursday and Friday evenings from 6:00 p.m. until 8:00 p.m. Elijah supports local up-and-coming disc jockeys from the tri-state area. During the Happy Hour set this week, DJ XaXa from Englewood, New Jersey, is spinnin' on the 1s and 2s. DJ Tra spins from 10:00 p.m. to 2:00 a.m.

"Stay for Happy Hour." Elijah insists.

I agree to stay, although I want to go home to Netflix and chill.

Yvonne appears, "Nikita, welcome back! Would you like a Manhattan?"

"Hi, Yvonne! You have a great memory! If I drink a Manhattan, I will end up over there on the bridge asleep. May I please have a Margarita instead?"

"Yvonne, you can bring Nikita's drink to my suite."

Elijah offers his hand to help me out the booth. I follow as we make entrance into a glass-encased lounge suite. There is an ideal view of the stage. In the suite, Elijah can adjust the sound on and off – moderate to loud.

"I didn't know he had a private lounge suite." Ivy injects.

Yvonne returns with a Margarita. She also brings a bourbon and a cigar for Elijah. "Would you like a cigar too, Nikita?"

"Now ya' talking!" I exclaim.

I stay well past Happy Hour – laughing, joking, and teasing with Elijah. He steps out every now and then when his staff calls. Repeatedly, checking in on me. "Are you good? You want a refill?"

"I've caught a second wind. I will have another drink since the live set is about to begin."

"Great!" Elijah orders me another Margarita. He sits down to drink his bourbon and lights up his cigar.

"Why is this man so damn sexy?" Ivy raises.

I take my shoes off to get comfortable on the sofa.

"Don't fall asleep!" Elijah teases.

"I won't!"

I am excited about hearing Bonita's set. The spice in her performance during sound check was incredible. Riding my second wind, I rise with a suggestive rhythm. Whine up. Whine up. I raise my arms above my head, playing in my hair. Elijah presses against me from behind. I whine up and dip against him. Elijah commands an app on his phone and the room turns dark. I can still see out to the stage. Elijah tugs at the zipper on my skirt.

"Elijah, stop. People can see us."

"We can see out but they can't see in."

"What kind of *Eyes Wide Shut* movie is this?" Ivy wonders.

"What if your staff needs you?"

"No one will bother us. Don't stop dancing."

My skirt falls to the floor and Elijah lifts my blouse over my head. I let the beat ravish me and I whine up harder against him. It doesn't take long before Elijah's pants are down. He spins me around and lures me to the sofa. Elijah puts on a condom and bewitches me from behind. Elijah pounds my ass through every drum, bass, and conga rhythm. Elijah pulls out to remove his pants from around his ankles. I rise and push him down on the sofa. I climb atop his hard penis. I nibble his ears, kiss his neck and lips. I stare into his eyes biting my lip. There is a burn between my legs. My clit draws heat from his penis. I clap on it. I look back at the blackout glass and clap, clap, clap on it. The cum seeps from my pussy. An orgasm rises and flows fast through my body. The surge travels up my legs to the tip of my clit and rests in the pit of my stomach. I can feel Elijah cum with me. I rode his dick like my life depended on it.

Then ... the moment of emotional intimacy sets in. You know – the eyes swell with tears.

I say it, "Baby! Are you okay?"

Elijah grabs my face and screams.

"Are you sure nobody can hear us?" I chuckle.

I dive into Elijah's chest as he laughs. Bonita exits the stage. The crowd is cheering for an encore. We dress and escape the suite to the elevator. The elevator ascends up to Elijah's office. We wash up in the bathroom connected to his office. The view from his office is worldly. You can see out onto the whole club. Elijah massages my shoulders. "This room blacks out too," he whispers.

"Oh yaaasss!" Ivy screams.

The midnight hour approaches. "Elijah, I'm going to head home now."

"Come home with me." Elijah begs. "The club is closing in a couple of hours. Stay up here. You can lie down and get some rest."

"We have two cars here. I'm not going to feel like driving if I stay any longer."

"You won't have to. You can leave your car parked here. We'll come back and get it tomorrow."

After a long pause, I oblige. I lie down on the sofa and Elijah returns to the club.

Elijah wakes me up at about 2:30 a.m., handing me a cold rag. "Nikita, I am done. Baby, we can leave now."

Elijah pecks my lips. "Thank you for staying."

"You're welcome." I express.

Elijah must have gassed the Range at 100 mph. We arrive at the loft in record time. I am exhausted. I just want to shower and climb into bed. In the bedroom, Elijah removes my clothes and starts the shower. The warm water caresses my tired body. I climb into Elijah's bed and knock out within minutes. Elijah showers and does the same.

CHAPTER 5 –

"Booty Call Bag & Swag Bag"

Saturday morning, Elijah didn't budge for his run or workout. We snuggled in bed until about 10:00 a.m. I can smell a fresh pot of coffee. I wash my face and brush my teeth. Elijah follows my lead. He pulls out one of his t-shirts for me to lounge in.

"That outfit is special. You did pack a booty call bag." Ivy teases.

Elijah is in the kitchen watching MSNBC. He pours me a cup of coffee. "Did you get enough sleep?"

I peek over my mug, "Time will certainly tell."

"Do you have any plans for today?" Elijah asks.

"Not especially."

"Great! We can stay in and chill. I will drop you to your car later."

We lounge all day – cat-napping between BET+ movies. Ms. Vela prepares us lunch and later a pre-dinner snack.

"Elijah, are you going to make it through the night?"

"I'm going to take a cue from you and drink coffee all night. That will keep me alert. It doesn't matter. Spending time with you is worth a little fatigue."

Elijah begins prepping for work. His style is effortless. Elijah's swag is complemented by suits from African American designers: Abasi Rosborough, Gabriel Akinosho of Albert 1941, and Southern Gents, co-founded by Fola Lawson. He always styles them with a crisp white shirt and sneakers. His weekend wear is by Ouigi Theodore of The Brooklyn Circus and Jerry Lorenzo of Fear of God clothing brands. Elijah sources his sneakers from The Sneaker Galerie, owned by a young and promising local entrepreneur, Nair Pettigrew.

Before Elijah and I head out to the club, I grab my sneakers and a pair of jeans out of the booty call bag and throw on my blazer. Elijah drives down into the club garage. He parks the Range and follows me to my car. He presses me against the car door and leans in with a kiss. "Drive safely and text me when you get home." Elijah hangs around until I get settled in the car. He walks towards the elevator but doesn't get on until I pull off. I beep and drive off. Once home, I text Elijah. "I'm home. Have a great night! Enjoy your coffee." I shower, plop down on the sofa, and shudder to sleep.

My usual #SundayFunday turned into a #SundaySleepday – I slept until noon. I missed church, my brunch babes, and three calls from Elijah. After I wash my face and brush my teeth, I brew a fresh pot of coffee. I dial Elijah. He answers with panic in his voice. "Nikita, are you okay? Where have you been?"

"Whoa! Is he overly concerned or overly possessive? Slow down, there is a yellow light up ahead." Ivy warns.

"Elijah, I am okay. I am at home. I passed out last night. I texted you yesterday when I got home. My phone was buried under the pillows."

"You must have been dog-tired. You are a heavy sleeper."

"Undeniably, when I am exhausted. Friday night must have drained me. How was your evening at the 'Z'?"

"It was good. We reached maximum capacity and revenue peaked. I was wired – drinking espresso all night. Then this morning, I got anxious and was worried when I couldn't reach you."

"I'm sorry, I didn't mean to worry you. I'm okay and well-rested."

"Did you pick up Zoe yet?"

"No, not yet. I will pick her up around three."

"Maybe you should get some rest too before she arrives." I suggest.

"You are probably right. I will call you later. Bye, Babe."

"Bye, Babe." I respond.

CHAPTER 6 –

"Background Check"

My relationship with Elijah is gaining positive ground. We are having mad fun getting to know all about one another.

Elijah's birthday is October 15th. Cue his romantic Libra nature. Elijah is thirty-five years young and is originally from Chicago. Elijah reps his HBCU, Del State, hard. His BS degree in computer technology is evidence why he has all those special blackout gadgets at "Z." Elijah pledged Omega Psi Phi fraternity in his sophomore year.

Elijah and his younger sister, Eve, were born four years apart. Eve works in human resources for the University of Chicago. Elijah's mom, Mrs. Martha is a retired nurse. Mrs. Martha still resides in their childhood home in Chicago. During Elijah's junior year in high school, his father, Miles, died of cancer. Elijah recollects spending Sunday mornings singing Baptist church hymns with his parents.

Toussaint, Elijah's fraternity brother, introduced him to Zoe's mom, Barbara. Barbara and Toussaint were co-workers at one of the local area hospitals. Toussaint described Barbara as a "Chocolate Brown Round." Elijah remembers saying to Toussaint, "Ok, so she looks good. Is she good for me?" Toussaint's response was, "You are going to be good for her. She always has a story about a loser she is dating."

"Hanging out with Barbara was fun. She introduced me to the real parts of Philly. It was during that time I realized Philly was missing a premier nightclub vibe. I began researching the real estate market for a commercial space. Not long after, Barbara told me she was pregnant. I wasn't ready to be a father, but I was ready to make my dad's spirit proud." Elijah recalls. "Now faced with the reality of raising Zoe, it was more important than ever to build wealth. Real estate became my building block." Elijah adds. "Barbara was careless with money. She cared even less about my real estate ventures. For Barbara, the dream is free. What she doesn't understand is the hustle is sold separately. Zoe became her hustle. Unfortunately for me, our relationship was a bad investment. Zoe is, however, a great return on that investment." Elijah confides. "Thursday through Sunday, Zoe stays with Barbara. Most of the time, Barbara pawns Zoe off to her maternal grandmother. It's sad to admit, but I won't share my real address with Barbara. I also fear one day Barbara will show up to the club and give me her entire ass to kiss." Elijah confesses.

Sometimes a person needs a listening ear void of judgement and response. Today, I was Elijah's listening ear.

Music is a universal language. When you're happy, you rock with the beat. When your state of being is sad or melancholic, you listen hard to the words.

"What kind of music do you enjoy?" Elijah asks.

"I'm open to different genres of music." I reply.

"Alright! Let's play a game. It's called Song for Song." Elijah suggests.

"One of us plays a song. The other has to play a song in the same genre. The only rule is we have to kick it old skool." Elijah explains.

"DJ KiKi vs. DJ E." I laugh.

"Ladies first." Elijah contends.

"Nope. Age before beauty. Although, you are foiinneee!" I affirm.

Elijah plays his first song to start the game ...

DJ E	DJ KiKi
"All I Need" Method Man & Mary J. Blige	*"I Can Love You"* Mary J. Blige & Lil' Kim
"Quiet Storm" Mobb Deep & Lil' Kim	*"Queen B@#$H"* Lil' Kim
"Fire and Desire" Rick James & Teena Marie	*"Meet Me On the Moon"* Phyllis Hyman
"Bad Habits" Maxwell	*"Tonight (Best You Ever Had)"* John Legend
"Public Service Announcement" Jay Z	*"Where I'm From"* Jay Z

Bonus Round	
"Lost Without You" Robin Thicke	*"Make You Feel My Love"* Adele

We play his game, Song for Song. Elijah leads each set. I stay in the same lane for the Queen of Hip Hop Soul, Mary J. Blige. We both take center stage during our song selections. I rap Lil' Kim's verse. I speed pass Elijah with Lil' Kim's *"Queen B@#$H"*. Drop the mic! I won that round.

Elijah grabs the mic for Jay Z's *"Public Service Announcement"*. I sway back and forth with my song selection in round five. My options include, Biggie's *"Warning"*, and Tupac's *"Holla' If Ya Hear Me."* In the end, it is all about where Brooklyn at, with Jay Z's *"Where I'm From."* I challenge Elijah for a bonus round. I don't know who is winning, but we are definitely jammin' and having fun.

A few weeks ago, Joie and I attended a sex toy demonstration. We played a game called the "Alphabet of Sex". The hostess presented a letter in the alphabet and we had to scream out words associated with sexual activity. Who knew there were so many words to describe the reproductive functions. I purchased a butterfly effect panty vibrator with remote control.

Elijah suggests I wear the butterfly tonight for "Talk Tuesdays".

"The remote will be safe here in my pocket." Elijah snickers.

"Talk Tuesdays" is a new intimate platform series he is testing at the club on the third Tuesday of the month. "Talk Tuesdays" is a community platform for local activists, creatives, entrepreneurs and local candidates running for political office. In addition to discussions about civic and social reform, entrepreneurs pitch their brand awareness, artists perform spoken word, and rock out during the jam sessions.

Brandy tags along with me for the evening. The event commences with a major topic of concern; the rise of gun violence in Philly. An ensuing debate calls for larger police presence and patrol near community parks and recreation centers. Young teens should feel safe to play a pick-up game and socially gather for fun. A stroll in the park should be a healthy retreat and not a retreat to safety. Some present a call to action for more funding and support of non-profit organizations who have demonstrated success in the transition from street corners to programs that offer skill training and job placement. Conversations relative to mental health awareness and police training initiatives to deescalate a situation without extreme force, took center stage. Several candidates running for local office cast their net for votes with campaign promises and measures for change and accountability. "Talk Tuesdays" has the potential to become a great model for the community to ignite change for a safer Philly.

Elijah is standing in at the bar serving drinks for Yvonne who is on break. Brandy and I are jammin' to a freestyle against The Roots, "*Ain't Sayin Nothin*" beat. Elijah activates the butterfly, flirting with my button. I jolt forward knocking over my drink. Brandy jumps to cover the spill. As I lean in to help

Brandy with the spill, another surge of satisfaction tickles my clit. I fumble the napkins in her lap.

"You are all fingers and thumbs tonight. Did you pre-game at home before y'all came out?" Brandy ask.

I look over at Elijah - his face covered in a playful grin. Elijah walks over to the booth to hand me another drink.

"You are mad clumsy tonight." Elijah laughs.

"I said the same thing." Brandy giggles.

I shoot him a look as he places his hand in his pocket. Elijah activates the remote sending me another tantalizing vibration.

"Elijah!" I flutter.

I clinch my legs together to gain control of my frenzy and mute my gasp. Brandy is puzzled by my erratic behavior. I was prepared to perform a spoken word piece I was working on, but in light of Elijah's fascination with his new toy, I decline.

"Gurlll, no toy story performance for you tonight." Ivy says.

All evening I felt butterflies and the desire to take flight home with Elijah.

CHAPTER 7 –

"Da Bruhz"

Elijah's bruhz are beautiful creations from above.

Toussaint stands tall with an athletic build, doey eyes, and fawn brown skin. His personality is large and his grip is strong. I don't know what Toussaint's grooming regime is – but his skin is smooth like butter. He was a linebacker in college.

Lavon's reach is statuesque. The reflection of light on his bald head makes his brown eyes sparkle. Lavon's smile will melt your panties off against his chestnut brown skin tone. He played point guard in college.

Charles' heart is as big as his arms and legs. His buttercup brown complexion and jet-black waves on a spin will leave you twirling. His teddy bear grip is warm and lush like his drinking skills.

"Bruhz, what do you see when you ride around the city?" Elijah asks.

"Dawg, is that a rhetorical question?" Charles asks.

"No. I see license tags from New York and California. Investors from out of town are making a big splash here in real estate. We need to ride the wave and invest in our community." Elijah replies.

"Dawg, my pockets are light. That last poker game set me back." Toussaint notes.

"I agree with E. We need to be playin' in the game of real estate." Lavon responds.

"Real estate is worth the gamble. Touss, I will front your ends until you are back up." Elijah adds. "We buy, rehab, and rent. We will each own 25 percent of each project. We buy in close proximity to college campuses. We also invest in dilapidated properties in areas where we can revive a black renaissance. Once we establish a portfolio, we can step our hustle up. We can create a management arm to superintend the properties full time."

"Be owt!" da bruhz bark in unison.

"Roo![5] Our first project is in West Philly. There is a triplex in the 'Cedar Gardens' area. It is a full gut Victorian with loads of old charm. Students and millennials will clamor to live there."

---

5   **Roo**, exclamation used by da bruhz, Yes! Yeah! That's Right! Thank you! Good job! Ok!

CHAPTER 8 –

"Princess Zoe"

Elijah calls. "Zoe and I would like for you to join us Sunday for family dinner." "No pressure." Elijah adds.

"Absolutely! I am honored to join you both for dinner on Sunday."

"I am not privy to what's on the menu. Zoe is planning it with Ms. Vela. I wouldn't be surprised if we weren't having cheeseburgers and french fries. That is Zoe's favorite meal."

"Do you need me to bring anything?" I ask.

"Just bring your smile. We have it all covered here." Elijah answers.

I am nervous about meeting Zoe. Mostly because Zoe is the center of Elijah's soul. Zoe is Elijah's lifeline – his heartbeat. Secondly, because this is a monumental step in my relationship with Elijah. After church service on Sunday, I make a stop at Target. I prefer not to arrive at Elijah's empty-handed. I peruse the toy aisle. On the shelf is a Princess Tiana doll. Princess Tiana dons a beautiful blue ball gown and a rhinestone tiara. *"Perfect!"* I grab the doll, a gift bag, and head to checkout. I arrive at Elijah's loft around 5:00 p.m. While still in the car, I have a moment of prayer with God.

"Hello, Father God. I come to you to ask for courage to be my authentic self. I come to you to ask for faith in love. I come to you to ask for hope, trust, and promise in building a relationship with Elijah. I come to you to ask for today to be a great day to forge a glorious bond with Zoe. Thank you, Father

God, for your grace and mercy. Thank you, Father God, for your favor over my life. Amen!"

I exit my car and enter the elevator. Elijah and Zoe are both standing to greet me as the elevator doors open.

"Zoe, this is Ms. Nikita. Nikita, this is my daughter, Zoe."

"Hi, Ms. Nikita." Zoe shyly mumbles.

"Hi, Miss Zoe! It is a pleasure to meet you. You are an adorable princess! I have a gift for you."

"What do you say, Zoe?"

Zoe reaches for the gift bag. "Thank you."

I lean in to hug Elijah. Zoe grabs a possessive hold of Elijah's hand.

"Nikita, let me take your blazer." Elijah offers. "Let's sit in the living room. Ms. Vela will call us soon for dinner."

Elijah and Zoe converge to the sofa. As I sit, Zoe watches my every move, staying close to her father.

"Zoe, I would love for you to open your gift. I hope you like it."

Zoe pulls the box out of the bag. Her eyes widen and a big smile flashes across her face.

"Look, Dada! It's Princess Tiana!"

"Zoe! She is pretty!" Elijah exclaims.

"Your father showed me some of his favorite pictures of you. I think Princess Tiana is as pretty as you are."

Zoe boasts a huge grin, "Dada, can you open it for me?"

"Yes, Zoe. I will open it after dinner."

Ms. Vela enters the room. "Hi, Nikita."

"Hi, Ms. Vela."

"Dinner is ready." Ms. Vela announces.

We all head into the kitchen. The aroma is inviting.

"Ms. Nikita, do you like cheeseburgers?" Zoe asks.

"I do, Zoe."

Zoe giggles, "Me too."

Elijah was right. The menu consists of cheeseburgers and french fries. Ms. Vela also tossed a garden salad. The cheeseburgers have a smoky onion flavor and the spice on the fries is savory too. Zoe's burger is sloppy. She loves ketchup. It is all over her face and hands. It doesn't stop her from devouring her plate. Zoe puts the french fries on top of her burger. Zoe has a prodigious appetite. The conversation at dinner is very minimal. Everyone is concentrating on their food. Ms. Vela is a great cook! You remember the bacon and eggs on the ciabatta roll. That sandwich was appetizing. Once Zoe is done eating, Elijah cleans her up. Zoe puckers her lips out for Elijah to wash her face. Zoe is a cutie patootie.

Zoe grabs her box from the living room. "Dada, can you open this? Pretty please!"

I adore children with manners. I can tell Elijah and his village are rearing a beautiful young girl. Elijah opens up the box. Zoe is in awe of Princess Tiana. I'm so happy she likes her. Elijah and I move to the living room while Ms. Vela tidies up the kitchen.

"Nikita, I hope you left room for dessert." Ms. Vela remarks.

"Ms. Vela, I will make room. Thank you for dinner. It was delicious!"

"Thank you! Nikita, I'm glad you enjoyed it."

"Nikita, would you care for a drink?" Elijah asks.

"Yes, please. A glass of wine would be nice."

Elijah pours a glass of shiraz for me and a bourbon for himself. Zoe is playing with Princess Tiana. Elijah sits next to me on the sofa.

"Thank you. You didn't have to do that for Zoe. She likes her doll."

"Elijah, it was my pleasure. Thank you for inviting me to dinner. I really appreciate you giving me the opportunity to meet Zoe."

"Of course. It was time for my princess to meet my queen."

I smile and caress Elijah's face. I want to kiss him but I don't want to freak out Zoe.

Zoe straddles my hand. "Ms. Nikita, you wanna see my room?"

"I would love to see your room, Zoe!" I wink at Elijah.

Zoe's room is fit for a princess. The walls are coated in cotton candy pink. She has a Lincoln Park inspired Greystone dollhouse. There is a corner dedicated to *Doc McStuffins*. Zoe has a nursery, hospital care cart, and a doctor's bag. She has a brass canopy bed cloaked in a pink and white duvet with white eyelet sheets. Her dolls are seated at a table layered with tea cups, saucers, and a teapot. Zoe plays well by herself. She has a funny imagination. Zoe introduces Princess Tiana and me to her other dolls. We sip tea and sing to *"Almost There"* from the *Princess and the Frog* soundtrack.

Ms. Vela peeks in to call Zoe and me for dessert. Elijah sets the Bluetooth to a Snoh Aalegra playlist. I love how Snoh Aalegra's sound is fueled with passion and adoration. Ms. Vela enters with a tray of strawberry shortcake slices. The cake is filled with strawberry puree and topped with whipped cream icing. Ms. Vela brewed a pot of my favorite Spanish coffee. I am in dessert heaven. Zoe sits at the counter to eat her dessert.

"Ummm. Ms. V, this is good." Zoe exclaims.

I agree with Zoe, "Ms. Vela, this strawberry shortcake is sooo succulent."

"Thank you. Now eat up. There is plenty more." Ms. Vela declares.

Elijah must have a sweet tooth. He consumes three slices of cake. Zoe eats one slice. She is preoccupied with going to her room to play with her dolls.

"Zoe, I almost forgot. I wanted to thank you for the picture you made for me. It is very pretty. I have it hanging in my office."

Zoe smiles, moving closer to her father.

"Do you have a big office like my Dada?"

"No. My office is small compared to your Dad's."

"I drink Shirley in my Dada's office."

"Ha-ha! She means Virgin Shirley Temple. Zoe loves a bunch of cherries." Elijah adds.

"Yvonne makes them." Zoe says.

"Yvonne does make great drinks." I reply.

"You know Yvonne?"

"Yes. Your Dada introduced me to her."

"Yvonne makes me laugh. She always tickles me. I pee-pee when she tickles me."

"You pee-pee? Ha-ha!"

"Ha-ha! One time I did." Zoe giggles.

"Zoe, it is time for your bath." Ms. Vela calls.

"Okaaay. Ms. Nikita, don't leave. I have to wash up and put on my pajamas. I will be back."

"Ok, Zoe. I will wait right here."

"Dada, stay here with Ms. Nikita. I will be right back. Okay!"

"Ok, Zoe. I will keep Ms. Nikita company. We will be right here."

As soon as Zoe leaves the room, Elijah ravishes me with kisses. Elijah grasps between my legs. His lips and tongue taste like strawberries.

"I have been waiting to kiss you all night." Elijah professes.

"Me too." I confess.

"Zoe likes you!" Elijah beams.

"Zoe is a cutie patootie! She looks just like you."

"You think?"

"Absolutely positively. She has your vibrant smile."

"Zoe is my favorite girl. She is the best thing I have ever done."

CHAPTER 9 –

"Summer in the City"

Every year, The "Z" Lounge hosts an all-white marquee event "Summer in the City." "Summer in the City" is an annual charity event to support Omega Psi Phi's at-risk youth program. The program aims to provide at-risk students from Philadelphia public schools with mentors, summer internships, and scholarships to attend college. Invites include legislative, judicial, and local government officials, non-profit executive directors, Divine 9[6] Greek affiliates, corporate vice presidents, key sponsors, and Philly's elite. Elijah and his team work extremely hard every year for this event. Stress levels are high. The buzz surrounds every corner of the city. Top DJs clamor for a spot. Elijah and Toussaint describe past events as owt! I guess you have to be a Que to understand what that means. I'm guessing past events were epic! Everyone wants a ticket. And this year, Elijah has a date – ME!

Elijah appointed Yvonne lead planner for this year's charity event. No one is more zealous than me in supporting a promotion for Yvonne to become general manager. Elijah could then spend more time at home with Zoe and me. Elijah is on tenterhooks coordinating plans for the event. He has also been suffering from insomnia during the past few weeks. RSVPs are coming

---

6   **The Divine 9**, noun, The National Pan-Hellenic Council (NPHC) is a collaborative umbrella organization composed of historically African American Greek letter fraternities and sororities. The nine NPHC organizations are collectively referred to as the "Divine Nine."

in quick. Invitations have been extended to my girls, and of course da bruhz will be in attendance.

"E.P.I.C. Let me hear you say EPIC." Ivy chants.

The rooftop deck is the main staging area. Elijah is presenting a check to his chapter of Omega

Psi Phi Fraternity. The donation is in support of the chapter's college scholarship fund. I'm so proud of him. I chose a white linen halter dress and leopard sandals. I had Elijah's linen suit pressed and of course he is wearing Stan Smith Adidas.

Ivy says, "Elijah likes Adidas because 'All Day I Dream About Sex.'" I'm shaking my head. Get your girl.

A red carpet embellishes the front of the club. Horns are honking. A parade of Town cars line 2nd Street. Philly's elite, grown, and sexy came to play tonight. Before the doors open, Elijah gathers his team in the pit. Everyone has a glass of champagne in hand.

"Thank you to all of you for your hard work and support of tonight's event. I want to extend a special thank you to Yvonne for her leadership. Raw Dawg, thank you for covering all aspects of security. Anthony, thank you for the catering setup, the craft beer selections, and the specialty cocktail menu. The city is counting on us to bring the "Z" Lounge flava tonight. The future leaders of tomorrow deserve a chance to be great. Please remain alert. Have fun and thank you for all you do for me and the "Z" family. Lastly, I want to thank my right hand. My darling Nikita for her unwavering love and support. I love you, Baby. Ok, "Z" let's get it. Roo!"

And so the party begins ...

Elijah, Yvonne, and I work opposite ends of the rooftop deck. Yvonne's hostess team is covering inside the club. We intermingle with local and government officials, key sponsors, and VIP members of "Z." I introduce non-profit executive directors to bank vice presidents and senior vice presidents. Community leaders, Divine 9 affiliates, real estate developers and investors intermix and network the room. The energy on the roof is marvelous. It is wonderful how the city came out to support Omega Psi Phi's at-risk youth program. Investing in a child's future and giving them an opportunity to go to college is a caring commitment for change. One of the best parts about this evening ... Elijah is smiling. I spot Elijah near the champagne float. He beckons for me to join him. As I get closer, I notice he is talking with a former colleague of mine, Dawuh.

"OMG! That askhole[7] is here." Ivy smirks.

"Nikita, let me introduce you to one of da bruhz, Dawuh. Dawuh, this is my girlfriend Nikita."

"Small world." I declare. "Elijah, Dawuh and I know each other. We worked together years ago."

I side hug Dawuh. "Dawuh, it is good to see you again."

"Nikita Brown! You seem to be doing well for yourself – on the arm of Elijah, King of the City."

"Dawuh, I don't know about the King of the City but he is my king." I brag.

"Dawg, this set is owt! Look at all these fine ass women."

"I'm good, dawg. Elijah replies, grabbing me closer. "Good to see you, Dawuh. Bruh, have a great time."

"Ms. Brown, always a pleasure to see you. Maybe later I can run an idea past you."

"Askhole, please." Ivy agitates.

"Dawuh, I'm sure you will enjoy yourself." I offer.

Elijah and I excuse ourselves and shift through the crowd.

"Babe, you seem agitated." Elijah cites.

"Elijah, Dawuh is special and always has been."

---

7   **Askhole,** noun, An annoying person who always seeks your input and never takes action or executes the plan.

Elijah laughs, "True Story."

Elijah and I join our friends. Lavon can't stay out of Nicole's face. Charles and Joie are absent from the group. Toussaint, Brandy and RiRi have an empty tray of shot glasses in front of them. Everyone is definitely having a great time.

"Nikita, it is about that time for the check presentation ceremony." Elijah announces.

"Babe, you got this!" I cheer.

Elijah kisses me and advances to the stage with Toussaint and Lavon. Charles joins them shortly after. The check presentation ceremony will soon begin. I stay with my girls. We're his cheering section. Dawuh couldn't wait for Elijah to leave my side before he pounced. "So Ms. Brown, how long have you and Elijah been dating?"

"Five months or so." I answer.

"WOW! Certainly, you must have put it on him. He is particular about who he lets into his circle."

"Interesting that he let you in, Dawuh." I scoff.

"You must be his trophy for these types of events." Dawuh injects.

"Dawuh, I caution you. Don't study me. You will never graduate, Boo."

"Nikita, the only lesson here is, you better keep it trim before Elijah finds another slim." Dawuh adds.

Before I could give thought to my actions, I slap Dawuh's face. I look up and motion for security. "Please escort this gentleman out. He is being rude to the guests."

Dawuh turns around to me and winks before he is escorted out. I hope Elijah didn't see that. Only the people in close proximity could tell what just happened. Right? Elijah's speech is going well. I think I'm in the clear. I down a shot or two and join the cheering squad.

Later Toussaint asks about my encounter with Dawuh. "Damn, Nikita! What happened? Do I need to handle Dawuh?"

"Toussaint, thank you. Dawuh was being Dawuh. I was not comfortable with his innuendos. I found his tone and manner disrespectful. Do you think Elijah caught that exchange?" I query.

"Yup! Knowing Elijah, nothing gets past him. You handled yourself very well. Remind me to never make you mad." Toussaint laughs.

"Summer in the City" was a huge success. Attendees dug deep in their pockets for a noble and worthy cause. In the entrance hall, da bruhz shake hands and extend their thanks to the guests. Afterwards, Elijah and I gather with our friends on the rooftop. Elijah hands Toussaint, Lavon, and Charles a Leather Rose cigar. Elijah proposes a toast to a triumphant evening.

"Elijah, thank you for inviting us!" Brandy exclaims.

"Yes. Elijah, the event was wonderful!" Joie states.

"Dawg, this event was owt!" Lavon remarks.

"Bruh, I agree." Charles adds.

"Thank you for the donation. The chapter really appreciates your support." Toussaint notes.

"Nikita and I thank you all for coming!"

"Congratulations! Babe, I am super proud of you!" I affirm.

"Thank you, Baby! I'm glad this year I had you to share it with." Elijah expresses.

We all proceed out to the valet area. Raw Dawg parks the Range in front of the club. We bid adieu to our friends and the staff. I take my sandals off as soon as we settle in the Range. I reach to turn on the radio and Elijah squeezes my hand.

"Babe, what happened earlier?"

"Shit! Shit! Shit!" Ivy squeals.

"Dawuh was brash with me. I did not appreciate his tone and insinuations about our relationship."

"What did he say?" Elijah questions.

"He said, I was your trophy for these types of events. He also made me feel uncomfortable suggesting that my sexual prowess is the only reason we are together."

"There is some truth to what Dawuh said. I feel like I won a tournament and you are the trophy. You are by my side at every event ... personal and professional. Yes, you did put it on me ... Darling KiKi! You know, sex is not the only reason I fell hard for you – you are smart, tenacious, caring, and independent. Babe, you slapped the shit out of that man."

"You saw that?"

"Ha-ha! Yes! I was centered on you to calm my nerves so I could get through the speech. I almost said 'Damn' after you slapped him."

"I'm sorry. It was not my intent to cause a scene."

"I hate to see what your right hook looks like." Elijah jokes.

CHAPTER 10 –

"Party for a Princess"

Z oe is turning four in a couple of weeks. Zoe influences Elijah's decision to host a "Zoe in Wonderland" theme party. Elijah enlists the assistance of Llona, a party planner he generally employs at the club.

Llona of "Lollipops & Licorice" presents an idea board to Elijah complete with tiaras, a bouncy cottage, teacup shaped cookies, treats, and a cake inspired by one of Zoe's pictures. Elijah plans to host the birthday party on the rooftop deck. It is September and the weather should hold nice for the party. Zoe invites some of her friends from school. Elijah invites a few of his frat brothers' children as well. Elijah's mom, Mrs. Martha, and his sister, Eve, are also coming into town from Chicago.

"I can't wait for my family to meet you." Elijah exclaims.

"How is the planning for the party?" I ask.

"All the details are complete. Zoe is going to be over the top with excitement. By the way, Barbara is going to be there."

"I figured as much. She is Zoe's mother."

My spirit is anxious about meeting Mrs. Martha, Eve, and especially, Barbara.

"This should be interesting." Ivy speculates.

The birthday girl is "Pretty in Pink" dressed in a tutu and tiara. Llona gifted Zoe with a pink rhinestone tiara. Zoe gleams just like a princess. The children are starting to arrive. Zoe and Elijah are expected in a few minutes. Yvonne serves Zoe's favorite drink, Virgin Shirley Temples. The children are mesmerized by all the cherries floating in it. I decide to meet Elijah at the club. My nerves have gotten the best of me. I'm thrilled to meet Mrs. Martha and Eve. However, I am indifferent about meeting Barbara. Zoe and Elijah arrive. Zoe screams in animation when she sees the tea party decorations and all her friends. Zoe runs to hug her grandmother and Eve.

"ZoZo, come give your grandmother a big hug. Happy Birthday!"

"Mom Mom and Auntie Eve!" Zoe screams. "I'm four!"

"ZoZo, you look like a princess!" Eve exclaims. "Happy Birthday!"

"Ms. Nikita says, I'm a princess!" Zoe mentions.

"Yes, Elijah. When are we going to meet this Nikita we keep hearing about?"

"Mom, you will today," Elijah reports hugging his mom. "Nikita should be here shortly."

"Wow! Bro, I haven't seen you smile like that in a long time. Nikita got you whipped?"

"Nikita is amazing! You are going to fall in love with her."

"Do you love her?" Mrs. Martha asks.

Without hesitation, "Yes Mom, I do!"

"Anyone is better than Barbara Batshit." Eve maintains. "Speak of the devil and he shall appear. Hell hath no fury."

"Well. Hello, Mrs. Martha." "Eve." Barbara grunts.

"Hi, Barbara." Mrs. Martha replies.

"Barbara." Eye rolls Eve.

"Elijah, what's up? Happy Birthday, Zoe! I see your father spared no expense."

"Barbara, what did you contribute?" Eve scoffs.

"Zoe, of course. Your brother, Elijah, is the entrepreneur. His pockets are phat."

"Dada, can I go play with my friends?"

"Yes, Zoe. Go have fun, baby."

Elijah's attention is averted when the elevator doors open. "Would you excuse me?" Elijah implores.

Barbara's eyes follow Elijah. "Who is she?" Barbara quizzes.

"Nikita! Elijah's girlfriend." Eve brags.

"Girlfriend." Barbara jeers. "Y'all know her? Where she come from?"

Mrs. Martha and Eve both ignore her.

"Babe, you made it." Elijah and I greet each other with a hug and a peck on the lips.

"I couldn't miss this grand tea party. How surprised was Zoe?"

"Zoe was super surprised. She grabbed her face in awe. She jumped and screamed when she saw her friends."

"I'm so happy for her ... and you!"

"Come. I can't wait for you to meet my mom and Eve. You ready?"

"Ready as I can be. Lead the way."

You know that feeling you get when your neck hairs stand at attention? Or when you feel like everyone in the room is staring at you and then you glance down to find you are naked. That's the feeling I had walking over to meet Elijah's family and Barbara.

"Mom and Eve, this is my girlfriend Nikita. Nikita, this is my mom, Martha, and my baby sister, Eve."

"Baby sister! Boy, we're only four years apart. Hi, Nikita. It is so nice to finally meet you"

"Hello, Nikita! Yes, we are so delighted to meet you. We have heard so much about you." Mrs. Martha highlights.

I extend my arm to shake Mrs. Martha's hand. "Hi! It is an absolute pleasure to meet you, Mrs. Martha, and Eve. Elijah raves about you both."

"Child, I'm a hugger." Mrs. Martha gives me a big and warm embrace.

"You did good, Bro." Eve grabs my hand and hugs me too.

Barbara clears her throat. "Well, Elijah, I didn't know you had a new side chick."

"Barbara, the only side Nikita is on is my right. And, I don't own a farm. I don't have no chicks."

"Nikita. This is Zoe's mother, Barbara."

"Hi" is all I got.

"Nikita, please excuse Barbara – she is ignorant." Eve lashes.

"Is that so Eve?" Barbara responds.

Barbara shoots her eyes upon me from head to toe. "How long have you two been side by side?"

"Six months." We both answer in unison.

"Zoe hasn't mentioned you." Barbara declares.

"I'm surprised. Zoe and Nikita adore each other." Elijah emphasizes.

"It would be nice to know whom my daughter is around."

"I'd be interested to know whom Zoe is around when she is with you." Eve scoffs.

"That is none of your business." Barbara huffs.

"Ok, you two. Behave." Mrs. Martha warns.

"Today is about Zoe. Barbara, curb your tendency to make today all about you." Elijah says.

Barbara's hand twirls, "Please Elijah."

Elijah looks at me, grabs my hand, and squeezes it tight. I squeeze back. I excuse myself as the tension rises between Eve and Barbara. "Please excuse me. I want to give the birthday girl her present." I kiss Elijah on his cheek and rub Mrs. Martha's back as I leave to look for Zoe.

"Elijah, really?" Barbara prods.

Elijah walks away, "Barbara, not now."

Eve rolls her eyes and struts to the bar. Mrs. Martha leaves to follow Elijah. Barbara huffs and walks in the opposite direction. I find Zoe at the candy bar.

"Ms. Nikita! I'm four!"

"Happy Birthday, Zoe! Oh my goodness, you are four years old!" I squat. Zoe dives into my chest giving me a big hug.

"Want some candy?"

"Oooh, I will have a lollipop."

"Don't eat too much candy. You will have a tummy ache." Zoe adds.

"Ok, I promise not to eat too much."

"Zoe!" Barbara screams. "Are you having a good time, Baby?"

"Yes, Mommy. This is Ms. Nikita. This is Dada's queen."

Barbara's face tightens, "Queen."

"Yes! I am a princess! Dada is a king and Ms. Nikita is a queen!" Zoe turns and runs back over to her friends at the bouncy house.

"I don't know why everyone is so fascinated by you. Elijah gets bored quickly. Don't get too comfortable – this won't last."

"I can tell you share the same fascination. Don't worry, Elijah is fully stimulated. You still wish you had Elijah! Don't you? Oh well. Enjoy the party."

"Bougie Bitch." Barbara snarks under her breath.

"Barbara Batshit." Ivy snares.

The birthday cake is in the shape of Zoe's face. Elijah provided Llona with one of his favorite photos. The likeness is amazing. We all sing *"Happy Birthday"* in Steven Wonder fashion. The DJ mixes in the 50 cent line *"Go*

Shorty, It's Your Birthday." Zoe jumps up and down holding onto her father's hand. Elijah picks her up to blow out her tiara candle. Zoe claps her hands and screams. Elijah gives her a kiss and a big hug before setting her down. Zoe runs over to grab Barbara's hand and then my hand – guiding us to the cake table. I cut the cake while Barbara hands out the plates. Barbara cuts her eyes cunningly over at me and I return with a wink and smile. Elijah shakes his head while Eve claps her hands laughing hysterically at the exchange between Barbara and me.

CHAPTER 11 –

"Family Dinner"

After Zoe's party weekend, Eve returns to Chicago for work. Mrs. Martha, retired, decides to stay and spend more time with Elijah and Zoe. While Mrs. Martha is still in town, I hatch a plan to host a family dinner. It is a great opportunity to introduce Elijah, Zoe, and Mrs. Martha to my parents. Ms. Vela insists on helping me prepare the food. We serve tenderloin steaks, yams, collard greens, rice, salmon, shrimps, and scallops. For dessert, Ms. Vela bakes a sweet potato bundt cake with buttercream icing.

Mom, Mrs. Martha, and Ms. Vela post up in the kitchen. The Philadelphia Sixers are playing the Brooklyn Nets tonight. Dad and Elijah retreat to the basement. Dad grabbed two "Ashton Majesty" cigars from his stash before he left home. He pours Elijah a Brandy before he begins his interrogation of him. Upstairs, Zoe and I play dress-up with my jewelry and shoes. Mom, Mrs. Martha, and Ms. Vela reminisce to old Motown hits, dance, laugh, and share recipes.

Mom later joins Zoe and I upstairs. "Miss Zoe, Nikita tells me you have a huge doll collection."

"I have Princess Tiana, Doc McStuffins, Barbie, and Wonder Woman." Zoe replies.

"They sound like a lot of fun. Nikita loved her dolls too when she was your age."

"Ms. Nikita, you were four?"

"Ha-ha! Yes, a long time ago, Zoe."

"You had dolls too?"

"I sure did – mostly Barbie."

We join everyone back downstairs. I can smell a brew of Ms. Vela's Spanish coffee.

"Delores and Jesse, Nikita is a wonderful woman." Mrs. Martha compliments.

"Thank you, Martha." Mom replies.

"Martha, you raised a fine young man too. Elijah is going places – doing big things. It is tough running your own business. You have customers, staff, and their families counting on you. It is a huge responsibility and pressure to be the boss." Dad adds.

"Jesse, thank you. I'm extremely proud of my son. Elijah and Nikita are good for one another. Lord knows, Elijah needs all the help he can get raising Zoe. Nikita is a positive influence on my granddaughter."

"I second that." Ms. Vela yells from the kitchen. "Okay everyone, come get some cake."

The moon glows in the sky like the bat signal. Zoe is tiresome and rubbing her eyes – a sign that it is getting pretty late. Elijah hugs my mom and shakes my dad's hand. They both move in for a bro hug. "You take good care of my daughter." Dad says.

"Absolutely, Sir." Elijah promises.

"Nikita, thank you for a lovely evening. You have a beautiful home. It is full of so much light and energy – just like you." Mrs. Martha comments.

"Thank you, Mrs. Martha. And, you are welcome. I'm glad you were able to stay a while in Philly!"

I hand Ms. Vela a bouquet of flowers, "Ms. Vela, thank you so much for all your help. I couldn't have pulled this off without you."

"Aww. Thank you, Nikita. These are beautiful! It was my pleasure. I had a great time meeting your parents."

Elijah carries Zoe to the car. She already fell asleep on his shoulders. I plant kisses on her forehead. Elijah skips back up the steps after strapping Zoe in her booster seat. "Babe, thank you for being an amazing hostess. I enjoyed meeting your parents. Now I know where you get your kindness and charm."

"You're welcome. I think it went well. My dad respects your hustle and my mom absolutely adores you and Zoe."

"Ok, let me get them home. I will call you later." Elijah grabs my waist to kiss me. "I love you!" Elijah affirms.

"Elijah, I love you too!" I declare.

That was the first time we both said, "I love you!"

"I love him too!" Ivy divulges.

CHAPTER 12 –
"*Barbara Batshit*"

You know the saying, "You betta use what you got to get what you want." Barbara wrapped her whole teenage and adult life in that cover.

"Baby girl, you owe me your life. Your father left. That no good son of a bitch left when I told him I was pregnant." Barbara recalls her mom saying when she was a teenager. "Don't ever give a man a reason to leave. You've got to give these brothers something to hold on to. One more thing ... Baby girl, don't just give it away. Make them pay for it." Her mother adds.

Every week, Zoe has a new Ms. Nikita story to share with her mother, Barbara. Barbara isn't too keen on the amount of time Zoe spends with both Elijah and me.

"Zoe, does Nikita live with your father?"

"No. Ms. Nikita has a colorful house. She has pretty jewelry and high heels. We play dress-up."

"You have been to Nikita's house?"

"A lot of times. We had dinner with Mom Mom, Dada, Ms. V, Ms. D, Mr. Jesse."

Barbara calls Elijah. "I don't appreciate you having my daughter around strangers."

"What? What strangers?"

"Anyway. Zoe needs some clothes."

"Zoe has clothes."

"She needs more."

"Then I will buy her some."

"To tell the truth, I will ask Tariq."

"Who is Tariq?"

"Oh, you can have a girlfriend and I can't have a boyfriend."

"Barbara, you can do whatever you want as long as my daughter is safe."

"What does Tariq do?"

"What does he do? Get money!"

"Ha-ha! Then why are you calling me for money."

"Whateva." Barbara huffs and hangs up.

The clouds peekaboo with the sun as the autumn breeze blows. Burnt orange and gold leaves gather on the windowsill of the loft. Elijah grabs a quilted vest and scarf before heading out to pick up Zoe.

"Babe, ride with me to pick up Zoe."

"Elijah, do you think that is a good idea?"

"Sure. Why not?"

"I don't think Barbara would agree."

"Who cares what she thinks. Besides, Barbara says she has a boyfriend now."

Barbara lives near 44th and Pine Street in the Spruce Hill neighborhood of Philadelphia. She lives on the first floor in a Victorian-style apartment. Elijah rings the doorbell and a burly man answers. He and Elijah converse for a couple of minutes. Zoe appears and hops through the door with her "*Doc McStuffins*" bag. Barbara follows behind Zoe and Elijah as they make their way down the steps.

"Why would you bring her to my house? Elijah, show me some respect."

"Barbara, show some respect for yourself. Go back in the house."

"Whateva. Bye, Zoe baby. Mommy loves you." Zoe turns around to wave.

"Hi, Ms. Nikita! Dada, why is Mommy mad all the time?"

"I don't know, Zoe."

"Ms. Nikita, you are always happy!" Zoe giggles.

"You make me happy, Zoe!" I confirm.

The following Saturday, I surprise Elijah at the club with an early dinner. Midway through eating, Raw Dawg, the security manager, calls Elijah in the office.

"E, we have a situation down here."

"What's up, Dawg? What's going on?"

"E, come down. Quick!"

"Babe, I'll be right back." Elijah hurries onto the elevator.

"Where is Elijah?" Barbara screams.

"Barbara, what are you doing here? What's wrong? Why do you have Zoe out like this?"

"Dada." Zoe cries.

"Zoe baby. Please don't cry." Elijah pleads.

"I figured I would find you here since you don't live at that damn bogus address you gave me. Here take her."

"What?"

"Zoe! Take her. Tariq said he doesn't want you coming to my house and disrespecting me. Since you and Zoe are so crazy about Nikita – you and the bougie bitch can have her."

"Barbara, so you bring her to the club? This couldn't wait until tomorrow when I came to pick her up?"

"Elijah, you don't listen. Didn't I say Tariq doesn't want you disrespecting me. Besides, Tariq and I are going out. My mother can't watch her. This is what you want right? You and your fairy-tale family. See if Nikita sticks around now."

I hear security radio for Raw Dawg as I am exiting the elevator. Tariq is trying to gain entry into the club. Barbara hears the radio call as well. She cyclones through the entrance hall beckoning for Tariq to follow. Elijah darts towards Barbara with Zoe clinging to him.

"Barbara, you're doing this right now – at my club?"

"Elijah, I have nothing else to say."

"You're choosing this man over your daughter?"

"Barbara needs her freedom from you." Tariq stupidly utters.

"Freedom from her daughter? You put her up to this?"

"Elijah, I make my own decisions."

"Man, go back inside your bougie club."

Elijah's teeth and fist clench. Zoe reaches out her arms for me. Raw Dawg is right by Elijah's side. Elijah moves in closer to Tariq.

"Girl, I hope you got enough funds in your money market account 'cause your man is about to go to jail tonight." Ivy warns.

Raw Dawg guards Elijah's way. Zoe's cry peaks.

"Baby, it's not worth it. She's not worth it. Baby, look at me. Baby, look at Zoe."

"Dada." Zoe weeps.

"Elijah, you betta listen to your bougie bitch. I'm out."

Tariq's tires screech as he and Barbara pull off.

"Barbara is batshit cray-cray." Ivy declares.

Zoe's sobbing calms with kisses and hugs from Elijah. Her face full of fallen tears. Yvonne whipped up a Shirley Temple with an exuberant amount of cherries.

"Why was Mommy hollering Dada? Is Mommy mad at me?"

"No, Zoe. Your Mommy is not mad at you. She is mad at me."

"Dada, I don't like her boyfriend. He is not nice like Ms. Nikita."

"Zoe, I'm sorry. Princess, you are with me now."

I'm glad Barbara decided to pull her stunt before the "Z" opened. Yvonne offers to manage the "Z" tonight in Elijah's absence. Elijah and I take Zoe home. It is a hushed ride home from the club. Elijah's heart is pounding and his palms are sweaty. We reach home and Elijah falls asleep cuddling Zoe in her bed.

CHAPTER 13 –
"It Takes a Village"

During breakfast, Elijah harks back to the events from last night with Mrs. Martha. Zoe sleeps in later than usual. I try my best to console Elijah, "Zoe is safe now. You can protect her." Elijah buries his head in my chest. He bellows in pain for Zoe and in anger for Barbara. Monday morning Elijah files a petition in family court for full custody of Zoe. I try to spend two or so days at home while giving Elijah and Zoe the space to grow in their new normal.

"I know you love your space – your sanctuary of silence and peace. But Zoe and I love having you here. My mornings are better when I wake up next to you. I love the arch in your back when you sleep. I love when you wrap your legs around me. I love when we build ideas together. I love when we fall upon faith to get us through. Is it selfish that I want more of you than I already have? What I'm trying to say is – here is an elevator key. You can come and go as you please. I hope you cum more."

"Ha-ha! Elijah, is that your truth?"

"What? I meant come over more. No I didn't. I meant what I said. Baby, cum for me, 'cause I love you." Elijah muses.

"Elijah, you are a complete fool. Ha-ha! Thank you. I enjoy the company of you and Zoe too. Yaaasss, Baby! I will cum for you – I mean come and go more." I laugh.

"Now I want to listen to some Regina Belle." Ivy pokes.

Zoe enters the room, "Oooh!" "Y'all kissing!"

We grab Zoe onto the bed and shower her with kisses and tickles. "That tickles." Zoe giggles.

Zoe, Ms. Vela, and I start our daily routine eating breakfast together. Elijah has a protein shake before an early run or workout every other day. While Elijah drops Zoe off at school, I usually read emails and check voicemails. Elijah and I generally have a late lunch if I have appointments in the city. My portfolio covers Greater Philadelphia, South Jersey, and Delaware; I could end up anywhere on any given day. Thursday evenings are dedicated to networking events, and for Elijah, the club's weekly operation begins. Ms. Vela and Zoe go to the library for kid's corner. Zoe also gets her pick at a new restaurant. That girl has a healthy appetite; she is not afraid to try anything new. Elijah promoted Yvonne to general manager. Yvonne is a natural born leader – the staff and guests love her. Elijah cut back his hours at the club. Now he can enjoy Pizza FriYAY! – a phrase coined by Zoe. On Friday nights, we Netflix and chill. We rotate who gets to pick the movie. Somehow, we always end up watching what Zoe wants. She loves comedies and action movies. We must have watched *Black Panther* a million times. Each time, Elijah and I notice something different about the movie. M'Baku leader of the Jabari Tribe is his favorite character. Especially the scene where M'Baku and his tribe bark at Agent Everett Moss. Elijah is always on cue to bark during that scene. He is a Que!

One sun-soaked Saturday, Zoe and I head into New York City for a playdate. We enjoy brunch at a garden bistro in Midtown before catching an afternoon performance featuring Misty Copeland at the New York City Ballet. Zoe is happily beat from the New York streets. Back at the loft, Zoe snuggles with her dolls during bedtime. Elijah arrives, shocked to find me settled in his bed.

"Hi, Babe!"

"Nikita! Hi! I thought you went home."

"I had a fun play date with Zoe and I thought I would end with a sexy play date with you. I can go home if that's what you want."

"No, that's not what I want. I am surprised but happy to see you."

I climb over onto his lap, "What is truly going on?"

"Given the circumstances our lives are changing, I'm wondering how you're feeling."

"Wondering or worrying? For life to be purposeful, you have to have a change in seasons. Zoe is good. Why aren't you?"

"I am good – when we are all here."

"I'm here. I'm in this with you and Zoe."

"Nikita, you do know we both love you."

"I do! I love you too – both of you! Now can you shower so I can get on with my play date."

I become sticky sweet pressed upon his throb, sucking his chocolate kisses. His embrace trembles in the balance against dubiety and certainty. Elijah must surrender his fear to reinforce his stronghold of faith.

"I love us!" I whisper in his ear.

Zoe is happy living with Elijah full-time. She excels in her school work and she flourishes in her imagination. Elijah is concerned because Zoe has not mentioned her mother at all. Barbara hasn't attempted to contact Zoe or Elijah. Children are resilient creatures. They adapt well when in a loving environment. Elijah seems to be adjusting well too. We enjoy bonding time at night during bedtime stories. Elijah makes strange noises and animal sounds – animating the characters in her books. I routinely assist Zoe with her homework and Ms. Vela does bath time. Zoe is happy!

Zoe and I attend church services on Sundays with my brunch babes. Every week, my girls and I look forward to pearls, praise, and eggs. On our way home one Sunday Funday, Zoe asks, "Why does Ms. Joie call you KiKi?"

"KiKi is the name my friends call me by."

"Can I call you KiKi?" Zoe asks.

"Absolutely!" I exclaim.

CHAPTER 14 –

"It's the King's Birthday"

With everything that's going on in our lives and the world, Elijah and I need a moment to restore, rejuvenate, and relax. I booked a spa weekend in Rittenhouse Square for his birthday. Zoe is having a sleepover with my parents to give Ms. Vela some extra time off.

"Happy Birthday to you! Happy Birthday to you! Happy Birthday, Dada! Happy Birthday to you!" Zoe and I scream jumping on the bed.

"Ha-ha! Thank you, Zoe!" Elijah laughs.

"Happy Birthday, Babe!"

"Baby, thank you!"

"Are you having a party, Dada?"

"A private party." Ivy smirks.

"No, Nikita and I are going away for the weekend."

"I wanna come."

"You are going to Mrs. D's house."

"Yaay! Ms. D makes the best choco chip cookies."

"She sure does, Zoe." I comment.

I chose the "De-Stress & Detoxify" package complete with an aromatherapy massage, facial, herbal body wrap, manicure and pedicure, wet sauna, lunch, champagne, and chocolate.

Five hours later, we are blissful, blessed, and beyond relaxed. Elijah and I both nap. I wake to find Elijah in a peaceful slumber. He is beautiful! I don't want to wake him, but I do want to arouse him. I pull back the covers and inhale his skin-soaked aroma of freesia and lavender. I swallow up his dark chocolate penis. I can feel the zealous swell of his supple and soft penis inside my mouth. With the touch of my lips, Elijah awakens. I suck and salivate against the shaft of his penis. His breathing expands and relaxes the tension in his upper body. Elijah attempts to push me away. Blood flows through his penis like an electric current. His body jolts when my tongue carousels his penis. My mouth squeezes and sucks harder against his lightning rod movement. Staring up at him, I tongue lick the tip of his penis. A huge smile radiates across Elijah's face. He raises his hand covering my eyes. Elijah delivers a clamorous roar.

Elijah pants, "Nikita, what are you tryin' to do to me?"

"Seduce you." I cunningly smile.

Elijah and I dress for dinner. I call ahead for the reservation and pre-order our food. For the entree, I ordered lollipop lamb chops, garlic mash potatoes, sautéed spinach, and a bottle of Shiraz. Dessert delights paired with a chilled bottle of Lillet Blanc and brownies drizzled with chocolate ganache and strawberries. The waiter tops the brownie with a sparkler and sings, "Happy Birthday!" We have a post-dinner cocktail of Maker's Mark 46 and decide to head up to the room. I am eager to give him his next birthday present. I splurged on a black tulle and lace balconette with a matching Brazilian brief from La Perla. "Nikita, nice birthday suit." Elijah says.

Modeling it for him, "You like it?"

"I love it! I don't expect it will stay on long," he adds.

My alter ego wants to wish Elijah a Happy Birthday too. Prince's "*Darling Nikki*" riffs through the speaker. Caressing the fullness of my body, I whine and dance through every guitar string and drum snare, my legs spread wide and my ass held high. The rock and rawness of the song drags heat between my legs. I drive my hand down the middle of my crotchless panties, fingering my lips and circling my insides. My apple orchard is slippery and wet. Elijah rises from the chair standing hard in front of me. Elijah's kiss peruses my skin. His tongue slides across my breast, down my stomach, and across my thighs. Elijah lifts my body and turns to slide me down on the bed. His tongue touches my lips. I can feel blood flow to my clit. Heat pulsates my insides. A moan rises, "Elijah." Elijah's fingers slither in and out my orchard. His tongue moves in a frenzy covering every part of my core. My moans sing like a hummingbird. "Ooh Baby. Yes! That feels so good." Fueled by fire and desire, I can feel the intense rise of Elijah. The sweetness from my orchard glosses his lips and tongue. I flip Elijah over on the bed. I suck the ripe juices off his fingers. My tongue circles his nipples, his chest, and belly button. Kissing his torso, skimming his hips, inside his thighs. "That tickles, Babe." Elijah laughs. I swallow up his scrotum. Gently twirling their fullness in my mouth. Elijah grabs for my locs. I lick up the shaft of his penis and twirl my tongue along his corpus. His veins bulge. Elijah's moan grows long and strong. "Oooh! Nikita! Baby!" My mouth consumes his foreskin, tip, and opening. I consume his penis – dick to jaw. Sucking and slurping against the thick of his engorged penis. "Baby, stop. I don't wanna cum yet. Nikita!" I suckle, squeeze, and pull – slobbering on his penis. "Happy Birthday, Baby!" I mount on top of Elijah. His penis is swaddled in the warm and wet lining of my pussy. I whine on his dick clapping my ass. His penetration is deep and thrusts deeper. I clap my ass on his legs. I gyrate and bounce. I gallop and bounce, sliding up and down his penis. I suck on his fingers, eyes closed, ass clapping. Playfully, I see-saw and totter on his penis. His grip on my ass tightens. My name roars from his lips. "Nikita! Nikita!" A fury of heat shoots from my stomach to my clit. I grab his face as my orgasm mounts. My clit is lit and my orgasm ignites. Elijah's penis is throbbing. I can feel the moistness in my orchard as he explodes.

"I'm cumin' Baby! Elijah! Baby!"

"Me too, Baby!"

I serenade, "Happy, Happy Birthday, Baby!"

Elijah roars, "Damn, Nikita!"

CHAPTER 15 –

"You glow girl"

I have worked in Corporate America for ten years. In previous entry-level roles, I've always worked alongside a large minority workforce. As I climb the corporate ladder, I'm generally the only African American woman in the hierarchy.

Rochelle Lawrence is CEO and president of Lawrence Consulting Incorporated. Lawrence Consulting develops corporate programs for Diversity & Inclusion. Ms. Lawrence and her team create dialogue and training for the benefit of an inclusive work environment. They address race, ethnicity, multi-generations, gender equality, sexual and socioeconomic differences in the workplace. Ms. Lawrence is seeking a new bank relationship and my department has been asked to facilitate a presentation.

I've been handpicked by the director of Small Business, Mr. Floyd, to make the presentation to Ms. Lawrence. I am excited about the opportunity but a bit hesitant. I question if I was selected for my business acumen or because of the color of my skin. You see – Ms. Lawrence is an African American woman. Does Mr. Floyd believe I have a better chance at winning the contract because Ms. Lawrence and I share the same ethnic background? I have four weeks to prepare for the meeting. I am overwhelmed by a plethora of feelings: fear, anxiety, doubt, and worry. On the other hand, I feel confident, calm, and faithful.

"When fear knocks at the door, let faith answer it." Ivy testifies.

Weeks leading up to the presentation, my team and I pour over bank statements, profit and loss statements, balance sheets, and tax returns. I read through customer testimonials and watch some of Ms. Lawrence's podcasts and LinkedIn Live. It is important we develop the best strategy for success – saving "Lawrence Consulting" time and money.

In one of Ms. Lawrence's podcasts, she explains why a commitment to diversity is important for any company.

"Diversity refers to the traits and characteristics of a unique workforce. There are four types of diversity: occupation, skill set and ability, personality traits, and personal values. Inclusion means that all people regardless of their abilities have the right to be respected and appreciated. Companies who are committed to diversity show they care about their team. People spend one-third of their lives at work. Diversity & Inclusion allow an employee to bring their authentic selves to work. Research shows ethnically diverse companies perform thirty-five percent better than the norm and nineteen percent experience higher revenue growth. Sixty-seven percent of job seekers say a diverse workforce is important. Acceptance and respect are fundamental to the core of Diversity & Inclusion. Does this sound like your company?"

"Oprah, watch out! A spell has been conjured for others to embrace their Black Girl Magic!" Ivy notes.

Stress levels at work have thrown my equilibrium off. Lately, I have been feeling queasy and unbalanced. I have not been able to keep any food down. Migraines are wreaking havoc on my concentration. Elijah insists I go to the doctor.

"Elijah, I will be fine. As soon as this presentation is over, I will be back to normal. I just need to stay hydrated and focused. Ms. Vela gave me some ginger to settle my stomach."

"Nikita, this is not good for your body. You need to see a doctor."

"I will. I promise. I will see a doctor right after the presentation is over."

My girls and I always have each other's back. We have mixed drinks about feelings. Lol! No, that was not a typo. We laugh, cry, and scream together. Sometimes at each other. One thing is for sure, we can agree to disagree and keep it movin'.

"Real queens adjust other queens' crowns." Ivy praises.

After church, my brunch babes and I check out a cute brunch boutique in Chestnut Hill. Zoe ditched us this week to go to church with my mom and Ms. Vela.

"Chica, how is Elijah and Zoe?" Joie asks.

"They are both doing well and adjusting to a new normal. Elijah's recent drama with Barbara has him feeling anxious. He did enjoy the spa treatment for his birthday."

"I'm sure he did." Nicole laughs.

"When is the court date set for?" Brandy queries.

"January 15th." I answer.

"WOW! That's next year." Nicole responds.

"Damn! Family court must be busy." RiRi adds.

"The stress of my presentation and Elijah's baby mamma drama has me cray-cray. My stomach is in knots." I mention.

"Quitch, are you pregnant?" RiRi asks.

"No girl! My cycle is present and accounted for." I respond.

"Girl, you got this! Your presentation is going to be #girlbossgreat." Joie cheers.

"What are you worried about? God has already conjured up a Black Girl Magic spell. Prayer!" Brandy adds.

"Lovelies, thank you. I know GOD got this." I praise.

The morning of the presentation, I woke drenched in sweat.

"This will all be over by noon." I tell myself.

I begin the presentation with our value proposition and team introductions.

"Ms. Lawrence, thank you and your team for your time and attention this morning. My name is Nikita Brown and I am one of the portfolio managers here at Paulstian Bank. I serve the business community here in Philadelphia, Delaware and South New Jersey. At Paulstian Bank, businesses like yours have the pleasure of a dedicated team of professionals to assist in managing your bank relationship. My team and I have shared success in financing growth, protecting against fraud, and developing efficient strategies to save companies like yours time and money. Today we seek the opportunity to become a valuable resource and thought partner for Lawrence Consulting. Do you have any questions before my team and I begin?"

"Yes, Ms. Brown. What does Diversity & Inclusion mean to you?" Ms. Lawrence asks.

"You glow girl!" Ivy cheers.

"Ms. Lawrence, thank you for your question. What does Diversity & Inclusion mean to me? Well, it is not enough to have a seat at the table if you are going to be silent. When I think about what Diversity & Inclusion mean to me, I recall the 'Motown' musical, *The WIZ, an* adaptation of the classic, *Wizard of Oz*. Dorothy sets out on a journey down the yellow brick road to return home to her family. Along the way, she meets a unique set of characters with different backgrounds and beliefs. They make a choice to journey together through the 'Land of Oz.' They ease into a strategic venture, fighting fear of the unknown to meet the 'Great and Powerful Oz.' Through their experiences, the Lion garners respect for his courage, the Scarecrow's value is in his knowledge, and the Tin Man leads the charge with his heart. Diversity is having access to the yellow brick road and the people you meet along the way. Inclusion is when you are given the opportunity to click your heels, use your talents and the best version of yourself to spark a 'Golden' standard for acceptance, awareness, and change. Ms. Lawrence, I hope that answers your question."

"Ms. Brown, thank you. It does. You may proceed."

The team introductions and presentation take about an hour and a half. My team is pleased and the grin on Ms. Lawrence's face suggests we did well.

"Ms. Brown, I must say you and your team have done your research. I am pleased with your presentation. However, I am extremely pleased with your thoughts about D&I. I have made my decision."

Everyone in the room gazes at Ms. Lawrence with mute appeal. My stomach is twitching. Ms. Lawrence rises from the chair. "Ms. Brown, Congratulations! Lawrence Consulting is officially your new client."

"Yes! Ms. Lawrence on behalf of my team, thank you. We are enthused about the growth of your company and this new alliance. Thank you!"

"Ms. Brown, you deserve my business. You and your team did well! Thank you. My comptroller will be happy about the annual savings and efficient solutions you presented. She will be in touch to discuss next steps." Ms. Lawrence and her team exit the office.

"Nikita, you did it! Congratulations!" Mr. Floyd cheers.

"Thank you all for your hard work and support. We did it!" I commend.

I excuse myself and hurry to the bathroom. My adrenaline has spiraled downward. I run for a stall and throw up.

CHAPTER 16 –

"Thankful"

I overheard Zoe on the phone with my mom. She said, "Mom Mom, I'm coming to Chicago with Dada and my KiKi."

Elijah laughs when Zoe says "My KiKi."

"Zoe is cute as a button." I note.

"You're cute as a button too." Elijah replies.

"I've never been to Chicago. What do you miss about home?"

"On the one hand, Chicago is pure and prosperous. On the back hand, Chicago is gritty, grey, tough, and devilishly windy. I miss the deep-dish pizza, buttermilk donuts, pepper steak and eggs, and Italian ices. The Italian beef sandwiches are similar to a cheesesteak. The weather is beautiful during the spring and summer and blustery cold during the fall and winter." Elijah recalls.

We arrive at O'Hare International Airport at 11:00 a.m. Thankfully, my parents and Ms. Vela made the trip with us. Elijah made arrangements for transportation to his mom's house. We pull up to a Classical Revival Greystone house. The limestone masonry is illustrious craftsmanship. The garden is rich and vibrant with purple, pink, and green flowers. The railings are black iron with crowned finials. Mrs. Martha greets us at the door. "Welcome to Chicago.

Did you guys have a smooth flight?"

"Martha, it's good to see you!" Dad exclaims.

"Hey, Lovely, it's so good to see you." My mother cheers.

"Jesse, Delores, Carla! Welcome!"

"What about us?" Elijah snarls.

"Hello, Nikita! ZoZo, you are getting so tall! Elijah."

"Really Mom?"

"Aww, Eli. Give me some sugar! Hello, Son! Welcome home!"

"Please come in. Drop your bags. Please make yourself at home!"

"Mrs. Martha, your home is beautiful!" I compliment.

"Thank you, Nikita. I have lived here for over forty years. There are a lot of memories here – good and bad. But one thing for sure – love lives here. Please everyone make yourself comfortable. I have lunch waiting for you. You can't visit Chicago and not have a deep-dish pizza."

"Pizza!" Zoe shouts.

"Oh my goodness. Look at little Elijah and Eve. Aww, Babe. You were cute and pudgy. Look at those cheeks."

"Elijah was a thick baby. All he did was eat. Eve was and still is picky about food. If she can't see where the food is prepared, she will not eat it." Mrs. Martha says. "Ms. Nikita, I understand Thanksgiving is also your birthday."

"Yes, I am going to be a year younger and wiser."

"I don't know about younger, Baby girl. Wiser maybe." Dad quips.

"Jesse, you are only as old as you feel." Ms. Vela says.

"Well, Carla, I'm old 'cause the double Es give me problems."

"Double Es?" Elijah ponders.

"Yes, Son. My knees hurt. I can't see. I can't get no sleep because I always have to get up to pee."

The whole room laughs.

"Ha-ha! Dad!"

"Baby girl, you just wait. Old age will come for you too."

"You are not getting old. Jesse, you are vintage like a good bottle of wine. Speaking of wine. Red or white?" Mrs. Martha laughs.

Elijah takes Zoe and me on a tour of his old hangout spots. We pick up Eve from work along the way. Mom, Mrs. Martha, and Ms. Vela go grocery shopping. Dad hangs back to watch golf.

The menu for Thanksgiving is grand. Mom, Mrs. Martha, and Ms. Vela are about to put all their hands and feet in this food. The menu consists of herb roasted turkey, candied yams with marshmallows, collard greens with turkey butts, string beans with turkey necks, three-cheese macaroni, sweet potato stuffing, garlic mash potatoes, lemon pepper crusted salmon, sweet potato pie, sweet potato cheese pie, honey and butter glazed cornbread, brown sugar and honey glazed ham, potato salad and ... a two-layer strawberry shortcake for my birthday.

"God is good!" Mom testifies.

"All the time!" Ivy adds.

My social media and phone have been singing and ringing "Happy Birthday" wishes. I am thankful for all the birthday love today.

"Father God, thank you for blessing me with this amazing orbit around the sun!" I pray.

"Happy Birthday, Nikita!" Elijah wishes.

"Thank you, Babe!"

"Here. Open it!" Elijah says handing me a red box with a teal bow.

"Ooh! Loulou! Hi, Loulou! *You are so pretty!*"

Elijah surprises me with a chevron quilted "Loulou" YSL pocketbook I have been fantasizing about.

"Yasss! Elijah, thank you! I love it!"

"I love you!" Elijah replies.

"I love you too, Boo!"

Amber and gold leaves are sprawled about the neighborhood. The air is chilly and the wind whips up a gust. Ultra-kiln firewood is crackling in the fireplace. Dad and Elijah's blood pressure is definitely spiking. They cheer one minute and jeer the next over the basketball game. Zoe and Eve are taste-testing in the kitchen. I'm just looking around in awe of this beautiful Greystone.

The mahogany wood columns and cornices are exquisite. The marble wood burning fireplaces are warm splendor. The copper ceiling tiles are breathtaking. The family photos breathe life into Elijah's childhood stories. This home is filled with love.

"Nikita, it's your day. Will you lead us in prayer?" Mrs. Martha asks.

"Let's all hold hands." Zoe says.

"Father God, we thank you for today. We thank you for the family seated here and the family seated with you in heaven. We thank you for the hands that prepared this feast with love. We thank you for your grace. We thank you for the Holy Spirit in each one of us. We are grateful for your prosperity. We are thankful for your kindness. In the Lord's name we pray. Amen."

"Amen!" The family affirms.

"Let's eat!" Eve claps.

The Thanksgiving itis is eminent up in here. Everyone has found a cozy spot. Zoe and I snuggle in a blanket in front of the fireplace. Eve is patiently waiting for dessert and cocktails. Mom, Mrs. Martha, and Ms. Vela are traveling again down Motown lane. Elijah and Dad take refuge on the back deck with the firepit, a cigar, and Bourbon.

"Mr. Jesse, can I talk with you for a minute?" Elijah asks.

"Sure, Son. What's on your mind?" Dad inquires.

"What are they conspiring about?" A nosey Ivy ponders.

CHAPTER 17 –

"The Block is HOT in December"

The weather has been strangely appealing for December. The air is mild and the breeze is moderately cool. 'First Saturday' celebrations at "Z" are like carnival in the Caribbean. Guests dance from dusk till dawn. The party is larger than life – the energy is vibrant and sexy. The night I met Elijah was a 'First Saturday' party event. Tonight, the "Z" Lounge is hosting their "Annual Customer Appreciation Holiday Party." There is a crowd of people lining 2nd street. The block is HOT! DJ Tra is spinning on the 1s and 2s. The bottle service girls are as ardent as the patrons are teeming with liquor. The "Z" is lit tonight.

With the custody battle looming, I'm glad Elijah is able to unwind a bit.

"This custody battle 'bout to get ooggly." Ivy states.

Tonight, Joie, Brandy, Nicole, and RiRi are in the mood for a twerk stance party. Charles, Toussaint, and Lavon are posted on the set as well. Everyone is sippin'. I mean dippin' – Lavon and Nicole always dip and disappear. In the blink of an eye, the vibe changes in the pit. Barbara and her boyfriend Tariq enter the club. Barbara and Tariq willfully make their presence known.

"Hello, everyone. Elijah, you remember my boyfriend Tariq."

"Hey, what's up?" Tariq utters.

I can see Elijah's shoulders tense up.

"Hello, Ms. Nikita." Barbara sneers.

"Barbara." I sass.

"You can come out to a party but you can't be bothered with your daughter." Elijah barks.

"Whateva, Elijah. How is Zoe?" Barbara babbles.

"She is wonderful." Joie quips.

"Who are you? President of Zoe's fan club." Barbara scoffs.

"No, I am president of Nikita's fan club. What's your name again?" Joie reads.

"This is a private section." Elijah interrupts.

Barbara kisses Tariq on the cheek, "Let's go dance, Baby. We don't want no parts of this bougie ass section anyway."

"Well leave, Bitch." RiRi hisses.

"Bitch!" Barbara gasps.

"You heard me!" RiRi snaps.

"Huh. I can tell we are not welcome here." Barbara jeers.

I divert Elijah's attention back to us with a kiss. He squeezes my hand and I squeeze back. Elijah exhales the tension through his shoulders, a smile alters his stern face.

"Shots! Shots! Shots!" Charles chants.

"Roo!" Toussaint howls.

We all laugh and raise our shot glasses.

"Crown down!" Lavon shouts.

"Lil' Kim! That's my song." RiRi screams.

There is definitely a party in the pit. Lil' Kim, in Queen Bee fashion, pours honey all over the party. The "Z" is hot and sticky. There are pockets of people all around having a great time. Both the dance floor and the bar are buzzin'. Yvonne is filling into her new role as general manager like a #girlboss. Raw Dawg and her security team are on high alert. The club is nearing maximum capacity. I want to dance but Barbara and Tariq are on the main dance floor. Elijah will lose his cool over one shoulder graze, bump, or mention of Zoe. Elijah keeps an eye on Barbara for most of the night. Yvonne senses Elijah's angst and deflects his attention commingling with sponsors and VIP members.

Later in the evening, I see Barbara stumble past the pit. She is hella tipsy. Barbara drags Tariq over to the bar, bumping into patrons along the way. Barbara's slouch is all over the guy next to her at the bar.

"Buy me a drink." Barbara demands.

"Isn't that your dude over there?" Mirko, a soldier from Brooklyn, asks.

Tariq is mad drunk and overhears. "Man, you got a problem with my girl?"

"No, it seems like your girl got a problem with you. Why is she asking me to buy her a drink? You broke? Son ya should pay more attention to your girl and less time running your mouth."

"What?" Tariq snaps.

"Your girl wants a baller. Son ya pockets must be light." Mirko taunts.

Tariq clenches his fist and raises his hand. Guests at the bar scramble. Raw Dawg, who is standing at the other end of the bar, runs over and clutches Tariq in a choke hold.

"Get the fuck off of me. Bitch, get your fucking hands off of me!" Tariq hollers.

"Not tonight. Your bitch ass is outta here." Raw Dawg howls.

Raw Dawg wrangles Tariq away from the bar. Barbara grabs her purse and follows the melee. Patrons move to the side as security rustles to get Tariq down the entrance hall and out of the club. Elijah halts his conversation and sprints past the pit to check on what's happening. Elijah follows behind Raw Dawg and her security team. They escort, or should I say toss, Tariq out of the club screaming and hollering obscenities. I hurry through the crowd of patrons lining the entrance hall in pursuit of Elijah. Raw Dawg unlocks Tariq from her grip and pushes him against the wall on the side of the club.

Tariq gripes, "I don't like this bougie fuckin' crowd anyway. You fuckin' punks. You ain't got no heat." Tariq runs down the street to his car. "Fuck that!"

Barbara snaps, "Elijah, you're a fuckin' asshole!"

Tariq is steamingly rummaging through his trunk. He snatches a red bag from the trunk. Moments later, he returns to the front of the club.

A patron yells, "Watch out! He's got a gun!"

Madness ensues as time paces in slow motion. Tariq raises a gun in the direction of Elijah. Raw Dawg extends her arms to guard Elijah, barking for people to take cover.

Barbara roars, "No!"

"Pop! Pop!"

CHAPTER 18 –

"Panic at the Disco"

"**W**hoa! I'm hot." Ivy wails.

The air is full of panic-stricken noise. Screams pierce 2nd street as people run for cover. Security yells for everyone to move back. People are pushing, shoveling, and spilling onto 2nd street. Elijah always has plain clothes cops outside the club. Immediately, officers approach Tariq from all sides. Security evacuates the front entrance of the club pushing patrons inside.

Barbara rants, "Don't hurt him!"

Officers tackle Tariq to the ground. An officer grabs the gun, a Glock 17. Barbara jumps on the back of one of the officers. "Leave him alone!" Barbara hisses. The officer whisks Barbara off his back, handcuffs her, and forces her in a nearby car. The other officers continue to wrestle with Tariq. Officers taser and handcuff him. Tariq is then shoved in an unmarked car. The wail of sirens riddles the air.

"Move back! Give us some space." Raw Dawg howls. "E! E, it's Nikita! It's Nikita! Damn! She got shot!"

Suddenly I hear, "Nikita! Nikita!"

Ivy murmurs, "Damn. We got shot."

Elijah pushes through the crowd. My insides are burning. The *"brnd. n3w"* t-shirt I have on says, *"Don't touch the art."* Tariq ruined my picture-perfect outfit. Elijah hovers over top of me. I can't smell his delicate, sweet fragrance. I can only smell burning flesh – my burning flesh. His face – Elijah's handsome face is fading. "Damn, Nikita. We're fading to black." Ivy whispers.

"Baby! Hold on. Stay with me. Nikita, hold on! Fuck! Fuck! Fuck! Baby, hold on. Somebody call a fuckin' ambulance!" Elijah wails.

"Here! Here are some towels! Press hard!" Raw Dawg instructs.

Red lights flash pushing traffic to a halt. There are horns honking and people cursing through the traffic jam. Elijah's voice is cracking, his brow sweating. After hearing the gunshots, everyone makes their way to the front to check for Elijah and me. The tension in RiRi's voice is boiling. Fear glosses over Brandy's lips.

"What the fuck? Where is that fuckin' bitch?" RiRi hollers.

"Nikita! No, not Nikita." Brandy cries.

"We need to whip that bitch's ass!" Joie grunts.

"Father God, we need you now." Nicole prays.

His hands over his head, "What the fuck!" Toussaint shouts.

"Dawg, did this really just fuckin' happen?" Charles barks.

"Bruh, where did he get the heat? Nikita! No! This is not good." Lavon belts.

"Ouch!" I feel a pinch and burning in my arm. My body feels like it is draining. My eyelids are heavy. "Waaaaaahhhhhhh" is the screeching sound of the ambulance. The ambulance is in a race against traffic down Spring Garden street.

"Stay with me babe." Elijah cries.

Brandy calls to wake my parents. Meanwhile, Toussaint phones Mrs. Martha and Ms. Vela. With the time difference, it is 11:45 p.m. in Chicago. Yvonne shakes as she tries to balance a bottle to pour shots for da bruhz. Charles grabs her hand to calm her tremble. Joie, Brandy, Nicole, and RiRi are en route to the hospital.

"Bruhz, 'Crown' may not be the answer but we definitely need a shot." Lavon stammers.

"Everything is under control. Be calm people. Drinks are on the house." DJ Tra yells into the microphone. DJ Tra pumps up the bass on Meek Mill's "Dreams and Nightmares" and the dance floor fills.

"What we got?" The ER doctor asks.

"Black female with a gunshot wound to the abdominal area. Vitals are weak. BP is 80 over 60. Her heart rate is 110. She has lost a lot of blood. Blood type is 'O' negative." The paramedic replies.

"Ok, get me a pint of 'O' negative. Let's transport her on 3. 1, 2, 3. I need an X-ray of her stomach and abdomen. Call the OR and tell them we're on our way. Let's move people." The doctor commands. "What's her name?" The doctor asks Elijah.

"Ni-Nikita." Elijah stutters.

"Stay with us Nikita." The doctor orders.

"Sir, you will have to wait out here. I promise to keep you updated." The nurse tells Elijah.

At the hospital, everyone converges in the waiting room with Elijah. Elijah is seated with his head in his hands, blood soaked onto his shirt. His heart is racing against the throbbing in his temples. Dad is pacing the floor and sweatin' profusely. Mom and Ms. Vela are on the phone praying. Mrs. Martha and Eve book a flight immediately from Chicago. Raw Dawg is giving a statement down at the station. My girls—Joie, Brandy, Nicole, and RiRi—are in the waiting room crying and trying to make sense of what the hell happened. Charles, Lavon, and Toussaint stay behind at the club to assist Yvonne with crowd control.

A couple of hours later, the doctor comes out to talk to my parents and Elijah.

"Hi. I am Dr. Patterson. Nikita is out of surgery. The worst is over. We were able to remove the bullet that was lodged just above her abdominal area. There were no bullet fragments. Nikita suffered a hemorrhage and lost a lot of blood. There is no damage to any of her internal organs. However, Nikita is in an induced coma. Now all we can do is wait and see." Dr. Patterson explains to my parents and Elijah.

"Coma?" Elijah yelps.

Dr. Patterson continues, "Yes. I am happy to report the baby is doing very well – considering the circumstances."

Elijah's eyes widen, "The baby!" He wails.

"Yes. Nikita is three months pregnant. I'm sorry. Sir, were you not aware she is pregnant?"

"No."

"Do you think Nikita is aware she is pregnant?" Dr. Patterson asks.

"No. Nikita has been sick lately but she thought it was stress-related." Elijah responds.

Elijah loses his balance. My father steers him to a seat. He buries his head on my mom, tears streaming down his face.

"Elijah, everything will be alright." Mom assures.

"Doctor, when can we see Nikita?" Dad asks.

"Nikita will be transported to recovery soon. I will notify you when she is settled." Dr. Patterson replies.

Elijah grabs for his phone to call Ms. Vela. Elijah can tell from her muffled voice she has been crying.

"Elijah, is Nikita out of surgery yet?" Ms. Vela sobs.

"She is. The surgery went well. We are waiting for them to transport her to recovery. How is Zoe?"

"Zoe is sleeping peacefully."

"Ms. Vela, thank you. Please try to get some rest. Mrs. Delores and I will call you if anything changes."

"Ok, Elijah. My prayers are with you." Ms. Vela comforts.

Dr. Patterson appears as Elijah hangs up the phone. "Mr. Alexander, Nikita has been brought up to recovery. She is unconscious. You may go in to see her now."

"I will let her parents go in first."

Dad says, "No, Son. You go in. We will be right here."

Elijah is shaking as he enters the room. The monitor's recurring beep answers to my heart rhythm. The ventilator's breathing tube extends from my nostrils. An IV pierces my vein.

Elijah's voice is raspy, "Nikita, I'm sorry. Baby, this is all my fault. This should have never happened. I need you baby. Zoe needs you. I need you to wake up."

My parents enter. "Elijah. Baby, your mom and Eve have arrived."

Mom strokes my cheek. "Aww, Nikita. Jesse, look at our baby."

"Mr. and Mrs. Brown, I am so sorry." Elijah frets.

Clearing his throat, "It is not your fault, Son." Dad weeps.

"Elijah, Nikita is a strong woman. She will pull through this." Mom says.

Mom lifts his chin, "This too shall pass. You are both going to raise a beautiful family together. Go and hug your mother. We won't leave Nikita's side."

Elijah leaves out to see his mom and Eve. At the sight of his mother, Elijah becomes vulnerable and sobs in her arms uncontrollably. Mrs. Martha and Eve huddle with Elijah in a warm, loving, and full embrace.

"Mommy, she's pregnant. Nikita is pregnant. Mommy, she's having my baby. Mom, why Nikita? I didn't even know she was standing next to me. This is all my fault." Elijah snivels.

"Aww, Eli. I'm so sorry you are going through this. Son, it is not your fault. The fault lies at the foot of the man who shot her. Nikita will pull through. Didn't you say you fell in love with her because of her strength? Now you have to be strong for her – strong for Zoe and your unborn child. Strong like you were for Eve and me when your father died."

"E, how far along is Nikita?" Eve asks.

"Dr. Patterson said three months. Nikita doesn't even know she's pregnant. She's been feeling under the weather for a couple of weeks. I kept begging her to see her doctor. She refused saying it was work related stress. If she knew—if she knew she wouldn't have followed me." Elijah stammers.

"Yes, she would have. Nikita loves you. That's why she was there – by your side." Eve says.

"I didn't even know she was out there. It all happened so fast." Elijah mumbles.

Raw Dawg arrives at the hospital. "E, man I'm sorry. Where did she come from? I didn't even see Nikita outside."

"Raw Dawg, don't fault yourself. Do not take that blame on. You had your hands full. It was chaos and commotion everywhere. Where the hell is Barbara?" Elijah yells.

"She is in a holding cell at the station." Raw Dawg replies.

Elijah angrily avows, "Barbara will never see Zoe again – on my life."

Yvonne arrives at the hospital. In the waiting room, she stops to hug Raw Dawg and Elijah. "Boss, how is Nikita?"

"Nikita is in critical condition. She is in fight mode. Nikita is hooked up to all these damn tubes. She hasn't gained consciousness yet. The doctor also informed me Nikita is pregnant!"

Tears well up in Yvonne's eyes. "Pregnant? What? How is the baby?" Yvonne shudders.

"The baby is doing well all things considered." Elijah says.

Shaking her head, "Tonight is full of surprises." Yvonne notes.

"Nikita will be shocked and surprised. I don't think Nikita would have followed me outside if she knew she was pregnant." Elijah insists.

"Ugh. Boss, this is Nikita we are talking about. Yes, she would have." Yvonne notes.

Hours pass and everyone takes turns checking on Elijah. He won't eat or drink anything. Elijah objects to Eve, Brandy, and Yvonne's pleas for him to go home. The sunshine outside does not give light to the somber shadow cast in the waiting room. It only causes more angst for Elijah worrying about Zoe.

"Zoe! I have to call Zoe." Elijah says.

Ms. Vela answers the phone, "Hi, Elijah. Zoe has been asking for you and Nikita all morning. Zoe is worried. Elijah, she senses something is wrong."

"Can I speak to her?"

"Sure. I'll get her. She's playing in her room."

A minute later, "Dada, where are you? Where is my KiKi?"

"Hi Zoe. I'm at the hospital. Nikita is sick."

"My KiKi has a tummy ache?" Zoe asks.

"Yes, Zoe. Nikita has a really bad tummy ache."

"When are you coming home?"

"I will be home soon, Princess."

"Okay, Dada. Tell my KiKi, we have some soup to make her feel better."

Elijah tries to maintain his composure while speaking with Zoe, "I will, Zoe. I love you."

"I love you too, Dada. Tell my KiKi, I love her too. Kiss Kiss."

Elijah breaks down after he ends the call with Zoe.

"Please, Eli. Son, go home and get some rest. Go home and hug *Zoe*." Mrs. Martha pleads.

"Yes, Elijah. We will call you if anything changes." Mom promises.

Raw Dawg volunteers to drive Elijah home. Elijah is in no condition to drive himself home. Yvonne and Eve tag along.

"Boss, here. I grabbed a clean shirt from your office. Change into this. Zoe will be devastated if she sees the blood on your shirt." Yvonne insists.

At the loft, "Dada! Hi, Auntie Eve! Aunt 'Vonne! Hey Dawg!" Zoe shrieks. Zoe jumps in Elijah's arms. "Where is my KiKi? Her tummy still hurts? Auntie Eve, you came to make my KiKi feel better?"

"Yes, ZoZo! I came to help your dad, while KiKi gets stronger." Eve replies. "Look at you getting so big. Give me a big hug and a kiss."

Ms. Vela appears and hugs Elijah. "I have been praying all day. Any news?"

"No, Ms. Vela. Nikita is still unconscious. They have her listed in critical condition." Eve responds.

"My heart aches for Delores and Jesse." Ms. Vela cries. "I made some food. Please, everyone eat. It has been a difficult night."

"I'm not hungry. I'm going to shower and change. Ms. Vela, are you okay with Zoe?"

"Of course, Elijah."

"Elijah, you have to eat something. I will stay and keep ZoZo and Ms. V company." Eve insists.

"I wanna go with you, Dada. I wanna rub my KiKi's tummy and make her feel better."

Elijah cries and hugs Zoe hard. "Dada, don't cry. Her tummy ache will go away. Mine always does. Doesn't it, Ms. V?"

"Yes, Zoe, it always does. Prayerfully, Nikita's will too." Ms. Vela affirms.

Elijah's phone rings. It is Joie. Elijah's heart thumps as he answers panic stricken.

"What's wrong? Is Nikita okay?"

"Nikita is awake, Elijah. She is looking for you." Joie confirms.

"Joie, please tell her I will be right there. Please! Let Nikita know I will be right back!"

"I will Elijah. Be careful. We will see you soon."

Elijah takes a quick shower and heads back to the hospital. Dr. Patterson is running some tests when Elijah arrives. Dr. Patterson exits the room to provide my parents with an update on my condition.

"Mr. and Mrs. Brown, we increased Nikita's fluid intake. The shock to her body is cutting off food supply to the baby. We want to make sure the baby is getting the proper nutrients. We will continue to monitor them both. Mr. Alexander, Nikita is still conscious. I think she is looking for you." Dr. Patterson says.

"Elijah, Nikita is certainly looking for you." My mom ascertains.

Elijah enters the room. His eyes are tired and weak from crying. My throat is dry and burning. I can't speak with this tube in my mouth. I want to tell Elijah how much I love him. Tears are streaming down my face. He grabs my hand as his tears fall past his cheekbones. "I'm sorry, Nikita. I'm so sorry, Baby." I try to squeeze his hand but I can't. How did I get here? What happened? Where is Ivy? She is very quiet.

"Baby, you are going to be alright. You are one of the strongest people I know. I need you to be strong. Zoe and I both need you to fight." Elijah says.

My body is numb and my eyes are weary. Whatever is running through this tube in my arm, feels sooooo good. I am litty. *OMG!* I am floating in the blue of the sky. I want to rest on one of these pillowy clouds. I am going to close my eyes and sleep up here. I wish Elijah could feel how soft and fluffy this cloud is.

CHAPTER 19 –

"Brunch Babes, Holla if ya Hear Me"

Although my physical state of being is unconscious, I can hear footsteps, voices, and the sound of galloping of horses. "Horses?" Maybe it's the sound of one of these monitors.

The first week in the wake of the shooting was emotional and strenuous for all parties involved. Joie, Brandy, Nicole, and RiRi visit with me in the hospital after work and on the weekend.

Joie's top hashtags are #ambitious, #disciplined, #stubborn, and #sensitive. She tends to believe the worst things will happen. Joie does not throw caution to the wind, but she will mount up when provoked. Joie is also an extreme foodie.

"KiKi, I told you Barbara was batshit cray-cray. Why in the hell did you go outside? Raw Dawg had it covered. Raw Dawg is a Viking. I wish you could have seen how she gripped Tariq. He was probably mad a woman took his manhood. Raw Dawg was a beast when she put Tariq in a headlock. He was shook. Shook! That's how I'm feeling. You're not supposed to be laying here. Elijah is shook. I can tell. He is here every day. Your mom and dad are concerned about his well-being. Quitch, glow up! We miss you! Girl, your skin is looking parched." Joie says slapping lotion on my hands and feet.

"Chica, what's up with my mani and pedi?" I wonder.

Brandy and Nicole are both nurturers which you can equate their enthusiasm and generosity to. They were born on the same day in the same hospital, a fortunate stroke of serendipity brought them both into my life. Their passions run deep down into their souls. Distress fuels Brandy and Nicole's drive to find their center. They inhale learning and exhale instruction. They both serve their community as teachers.

"OMG! Remember our first girls trip to New Orleans." Brandy recalls. "Beignets, coffee, art, and music. Nikita, I know you remember that delicious crawfish etouffee and that Voodoo beer!"

"Yes! KiKi, you wanted to go to every art gallery in the French Quarters. You bought your first piece of art 'Pretty Eyes.' Honey, your hair is starting to look disheveled like the little girl in that painting. You need some of my twist action." Nicole says twisting my hair.

"Does my hair look that bad?" I ponder.

RiRi stands like a soldier – loyal and protective. She sits back and observes everything and everybody. Like Joie, RiRi has a funny sense of humor. Can't nobody match her street smarts and keen intuition.

"I told you Barbara was going to be a problem. I'm going to knock the bitch out the first chance I get. I was a little leery of Elijah in the beginning. He reminded me of that guy I dated, Caleb. Caleb was generous but possessive. He was fun and loved to spend money on a good time. But Elijah is different. Something powerful drew him to you in that club. Elijah is trying his best to cope. We all are. Stinka butt, pull up your big girl panties and wake the fuck up! We got a bitch to beat down." RiRi commands.

"OMG! RiRi, remember that time you whipped that girl's ass on Delaware Avenue? Now I don't condone violence but that was epic. She never talked gritty about you again." My subconscious recalls.

"I appreciate you taking care of Nikita. I'm sorry to have to put you through this. Barbara is my problem. Her actions are unforgivable. I love your girl, very much. I can't stand to see her laying in this hospital – helpless. I hope Nikita knows she is not alone." Elijah confides.

"Elijah, we know how much you love Nikita. She will wake up. You have to take care of yourself now so you can take care of her later. Go home and get some rest. Give Zoe a big hug and a kiss from all us." Brandy suggests.

"Elijah, I'm telling you now. Barbara thinks KiKi is a bougie bitch. Well, Barbara is going to be a beatdown bitch. 'Cause I'm coming for her." RiRi yells.

"Oh! I'm right there with you Ri." Joie adds.

"Oh my! Y'all going to jail." I sleeplessly inject.

CHAPTER 20 –

"Trauma Tells a Story"

"**E**ve, I appreciate you and Mom being here." Elijah says.

"Of course. As soon as Toussaint called, Mommy and I booked a flight." Eve replies.

"I remember the day when Dad died." Elijah details.

"Early that morning, Dad said, "E, please forgive me. This is God's plan. God wants me to join him in heaven so that you may grow into a man here on earth. You will become the man of the house. You must serve to protect your mother and my little angel, Eve. It will rain and pour, but you will be their sunshine and rainbow. God doesn't put anything on you that your spirit can't handle. Love with your soul. There will one day be a spirit that strengthens you." Elijah recalls.

"Wow! E, I never knew that. You remind me of Dad. One of your greatest strengths is how you care about people. I see it in how you treat your team. I saw it when you tried to make it work with Barbara. I see it in the way you are raising ZoZo. I see it in your eyes when you are with Nikita. You helped raise me. Elijah, I love you for always being there for me. You always make time for me. You always listen without judgement. Mom and I never would have made it through those difficult times without you." Eve confesses.

"Eve, I love you! I thought Barbara was the spirit Dad was talking about. I tried to save her from herself. You can't save someone who doesn't think they are drowning. The spirit Dad was talking about is Nikita. Eve, I couldn't save her. I didn't protect her. I put Nikita in harm's way."

"God saved her, Elijah. God protected your baby. Nikita was outside to make sure you were safe. This is not on you. What did Dad say? God doesn't put anything on you that your spirit can't handle."

"Eve, you did turn out pretty decent!" Elijah jokes.

Swatting at Elijah's arm, "Really dude?" Eve responds.

"Women come and go every night at the club. Touss always says, 'E, you can pick anyone you want.' The night Nikita entered the club, I was in my office. I saw Nikita and her girls come in. She looked up and smiled. Eve, I know it sounds crazy but her smile radiated so bright and it made me smile. Eve, I knew I had to talk to her. I wanted to know if her vibe shared the same aura and energy her smile did. Nikita was funny during our first encounter. I remember her cute laugh and firm handshake like it was yesterday." Elijah continues.

"Nikita does bring out the best in you. I can tell you bring out the best of her too."

I claim victory over God's promise and wake to see this beautiful but broken man. Elijah's eyes scan over a promissory note next to my bed. He and da bruhz secured a triplex in North Philadelphia off of Carlisle Street. It will be a great rental for Temple University students. The volume on the blood pressure monitor increases. Elijah looks up at the monitor and over at me. "Nikita! Baby! Hi, *beautiful!*" He jumps up, "Let me get your doctor." Elijah says.

"Hello, Ms. Brown. I'm Dr. Patterson. I am certainly glad to see your beautiful brown eyes.

I'm going to check your vitals now."

I feel weird – like something has taken over my body. The sound of galloping horses trots along one of the monitors.

"Nikita, your blood pressure and heart rate are holding steady. Your body needed a resting period. Your recovery is an important step now. I will have a nurse come in and get you more comfortable." Dr. Patterson states.

Elijah pulls his chair closer and clutches my hand. I stare at Elijah and then look over at the horse monitor. Elijah's eyes swell with tears. I want to comfort him, "Please, Elijah, don't cry."

"Nikita." Elijah's voice trembling. "It's a heartbeat. Nikita, that's our baby's heartbeat."

My eyes grow curious.

"Yes, our baby. Nikita, you are pregnant!"

"Pregnant?" I can hear my words, but I can't speak them. Tears trail heavy down my face. Elijah squeezes my hand. I don't have the motor skills to squeeze back. My thoughts tumble about in my head. "*I'm pregnant? I didn't have a nervous stomach? I'm having a baby. I'm going to be someone's mother. I'm having Elijah's baby. Zoe is going to be a big sister. Elijah and I are having a baby!*" Elijah kisses my dimple-soaked tears.

Over the next couple of days I start to feel better – stronger. I am staring at the doppler fetal monitor, shocked at the enormity of my baby surviving me getting shot. My vital records show great improvement. Dr. Patterson orders the removal of my breathing tube. A dry mouth and throat are comparable to the grit and abrasiveness of sandpaper. The nurse slightly raises my head and holds a straw up to my mouth. The water cascades down my scratchy throat. It feels like running through a water hydrant on a sweltering hot day. I choke and Nicole cuts her eye at the nurse. The nurse says, "Take your time." Easy for you to say – my mouth tastes and feels like I have been stranded for weeks in the Sahara Desert.

After about a week, it doesn't hurt as much to swallow. I want some real food. I'm so over chicken broth and Jell-O. Elijah painstakingly gives me a recap of what happened that fatal night at "Z." Tariq was charged with two counts of reckless endangerment, unlawful possession of a firearm, unlawful discharge, violating probation, and disorderly conduct. For weeks, Barbara has been blowing up Elijah's phone. Unhesitatingly, Eve blocked her number. Elijah is too vulnerable to deal with her BS. Elijah filed a restraining order and accelerated proceedings for full custody of Zoe. Barbara is contesting the full custody petition. Elijah hung a picture by my bed Zoe drew of a park with trees, flowers, and ducks swimming in a pond. Zoe desperately wants to come visit me at the hospital. Elijah and the family think it best she waits until I come home. Zoe calls me before going to bed. Zoe and I recite her bedtime prayer together.

"Now I lay me down to sleep, I pray to the Lord my soul to keep. If I should die before I wake, I pray to the Lord my soul to take."

CHAPTER 21 –

"What I Miss"

The good news is, I passed all of my conditioning tests. On to even greater news, Dr. Patterson agreed to sign my discharge papers. All praise to God, I will be released from the hospital by the end of the week. I was prayerful about being home for the holidays.

Dr. Patterson prescribes a tall order of dos and don'ts for a full recovery. Dr. Patterson also advises a strict pregnancy diet to increase my iron level. I'm pregnant – I thought I could eat whatever I desire. Elijah and Brandy arrive early to pack up my get-well cards and flowers. Increasingly alarming is the fact that Elijah has been distant with me for several days. Maybe it's because his mind is preoccupied with a whole host of other problems and challenges. He won't even make direct eye contact with me. While being wheeled out, I extend my thanks to Dr. Patterson and the nursing staff for their superior care. I must remember to ask Brandy to send them an edible arrangement.

The drive to the loft is wordless, as if we were each driving alone. Sitting in the backseat of the Range, I catch a glimpse of Elijah staring at me through the rear view mirror. When I look up at him, he cuts his eyes back to the road. I thereupon hesitate in asking him what is wrong. Moreover, there are still no musings from Ivy. Whatever Ivy is feeling, Elijah is feeling it too.

I welcome our arrival at the loft with anxiety and cheer. I flash a big grin as the elevator doors open. Everyone yells, "Welcome Home!"

"Thank you! It is good to be home."

Zoe is front and center with a joyous smile. "KiKi, I missed you."

"Zoe, I missed you too. Give me a big hug. Oooh!"

"Your tummy still hurts?"

"Yes, Zoe, just a little bit."

Ms. Vela, Mrs. Martha, and Mom have a spread laid out. Damn! As I recall, I'm on a strict pregnancy diet.

"Thank you all for being here and for supporting Elijah, Zoe, and my family."

Elijah braces my arm and ushers me to the sofa. He still doesn't look at me. He settles me down on the sofa and drapes a blanket across my legs. In haste, Elijah turns away from me and walks to the kitchen. Thankfully, no one calls attention to the tear swell in my eyes. I pat my eyes dry quickly with my sweater. I'm struggling with social conversation. Fatigue, tenderness, pain, and swelling interrupt my thoughts.

An hour passes before I excuse myself. "My apologies, I am sapped. Please, excuse me?"

"Yes, of course. You have been through a lot. We all understand, you deserve rest." Mom says.

Elijah steadies me on my feet to lift my legs up across his arms. He carries me down the hall to the bedroom. I rest my head against his chest. I can hear the steadfast rhythm of his heartbeat. Damn! I missed him and his delicious smell. Elijah helps me get into the bed. He carefully removes my sweater. "Do you need anything?" He asks.

"No, thank you. I'm fine. I'm just exhausted."

Elijah shoots me a quick glare. "Get some rest." His exit is quick - no kiss, no hug, nothing. My cheeks settle in a puddle of tears on the pillow. Later, the music fades and the laughter and chatter ceases. The elevator doors open and close a growing number of times. My mom and dad appear at the bedroom door to bid me good night.

"Nikita, we are calling it a night. We want you to know how much we love you. We are grateful for your recovery and excited about becoming grandparents. Please, don't exert too much on yourself. Rest and take time for you and the baby. Be sure to talk with Elijah. He has been by your side the whole time and I don't think he has come to grips with what happened." Mom says.

"I love you both very much. I know the last few weeks have been emotionally draining for everyone. I can tell Elijah has a lot on his mind. I pray he lets me in. I am excited but increasingly nervous about becoming a mother. I am thankful to God for my recovery too."

"Baby girl, I love you! You will be an amazing mom – like your mom." My dad says leaning over to kiss my forehead.

"Your father is right, Nikita! We will check in on you tomorrow to see how you are feeling." Mom notes.

"Be safe driving home." I add.

Before Ms. Vela readies Zoe for bed, Zoe peeks open the bedroom door.

"KiKi, it's my bedtime. I want to kiss kiss good night. I'm glad your home. Dada has been sad. He can be happy now."

"Zoe, I missed you. I'm glad to be home. I was sad too. I'm happy to be home with you and your dad. I love you!"

"I love you too! Night night!"

"Nikita, I'm glad you're home too. You gave us quite a scare." Ms. Vela notes.

"Ms. Vela, thank you! Thank you for caring for Mom and Mrs. Martha. Elijah, Zoe, and I love you!"

"You're welcome! Your mom, Martha, and I took care of each other. I love you all too!"

"Ms. Vela, is Elijah okay? He is very quiet. Distant almost."

"Elijah was painfully worried about you. He blames himself. Elijah will come around now that you are home."

"Thank you, Ms. Vela."

I anxiously wait for Elijah to come to bed. I long to feel the warmth and serenity of his arms wrapped around me. I want to express how much I missed him; I want to tell him how thankful I am for his presence and patience during my hospital stay. The passage of time toils in the absence of Elijah. Damn! Come to think of it, there is still no introspection from Ivy. It feels like the calm before a storm in the loft. *"Shit, I got shot! Shouldn't it feel like nirvana."* I slide off the bed and hover close to the wall for support. In the still of darkness, I find Elijah seated in the study with a drink in his hand. His head turns swiftly, "What the hell are you doing out of bed?" Elijah yells. A raging tempest dilates his pupils. *"Whoa! Who is this stranger in the loft?"*, my head spins. Elijah has never hailed his voice at me. A rain of tears falls down my face in an instant.

"What have I done? Why are you mad at me? Why are you being so short with me? Why won't you look at me for more than five seconds?"My hands wrap around my stomach as I slouch over in pain. My faith fades into the abyss giving way to infinite fear. "Oh my! I am an idiot! It all makes sense! You are mad at me! You don't want this baby! You are not happy about this pregnancy! You are mad at me ... for being pregnant!" I argue.

Elijah fumbles his drink down on the table and hurries towards me.

"Nikita! Baby! No! I'm sorry!"

My hand extends to halt him from coming closer. I stumble backwards.

"No! Don't come near me!" I yell.

"Nikita!" Elijah catches me. "Please come sit down. Nikita! Please!"

Livid with anger, my physical extremities make it difficult to back away from Elijah. I am forced to grab his arm. He lifts me and carries me to the sofa.

"Nikita, I'm sorry for raising my voice. I'm not mad at you. How could I be mad at you? I'm mad at myself. Baby, I'm sorry. I'm mad for not being able to protect you. I could have lost you. Zoe and I could have lost you. I should have known you were there. I should have known you were at my side. You are always at my side. Nikita, the best thing about all this ... we are having a baby. I will have full custody of Zoe soon. We are starting our own family." Elijah thumbs the tears from under my eyes. "Nikita, I am excited about the baby!" Fervent is his kiss. His zealousness rose at the same place it had fallen. "Nikita, I am sorry. I love you!" His kisses across my belly show adoration for our baby. He grazes my wound with a light touch of kisses. I can feel his warm tears puddle on my stomach. The cadence with which Elijah's heart beats reassures me of God's cover. I can testify, there are rainbows after a storm.

"Gurlll, I thought we were gonna be outchea a single parent." Ivy belts.

"Quitch, where have you been?" My thoughts query.

"I was asleep! You do know we got shot! For weeks, I have been attached to a morphine drip. I was dormant and high. Floating in the clouds – high up in them clouds. But, I'm back now. What I miss?" Ivy returns.

CHAPTER 22 –

"Every Perfect Gift Is from Above"

We have been tight-lipped about the pregnancy in the presence of Zoe. With the holidays approaching, my spirit is sledding through snow drifts on Christmas to share the news. I hope and pray Zoe is delighted about being a big sister.

"Babe, what do you think about getting Zoe a t-shirt that reads "Big Sister" and a new doll baby?" I ask.

"I think that's a cute idea. Are you worried about how Zoe will react and feel about the baby?"

"Zoe is happy you're home. She'll be happy about a brother or sister too. Zoe loves you – very much."

"I know. I just want her to always be happy."

"Isn't that what every parent wants for their child? Everyone except Barbara."

"We haven't talked much about the custody hearing. How are you feeling?"

"I just want it to be over. Zoe needs stability. Do you know she hasn't once asked for her mother? I wonder how she actually feels."

"Do you think she will share her feelings with the judge?"

"I hope so. The judge said she always has a one-on-one with the child before she makes her final ruling."

"Even though Zoe is four years old, she is quite a precocious child. Her comments always surprise us. Zoe is as clever as she is smart. It is good of the judge to give her the freedom and the opportunity to express her feelings. Zoe takes after you; she knows what she wants."

"Zoe does amaze me. She always finds the right words to make me feel better. Zoe was my nurturer while you were in the hospital. She made sure I had food to take to the hospital. She slept in my bed every night. Zoe said she didn't want me to be lonely."

"Hopelessness and loneliness are heavy burdens to carry. I'm glad you were not alone."

"Babe, I'm sorry. I grew more and more despondent after each passing day in the hospital. It was just every time I saw you in that hospital bed, images of you lying on the ground unconscious and bleeding wrecked my soul. I couldn't protect you. When the doctor told me you were pregnant, I was angry with you. You promised me you were going to see your doctor. I thought, 'Maybe if you knew you were pregnant, you wouldn't have run outside.'"

"I doubt it. When you ran after Raw Dawg, my intuition was to run after you. I wanted to make sure you weren't going to do anything crazy. I never thought Tariq was going to bring the heat. Literally! My insides felt like what I imagine hot lava feels like. What the inside of a firepit feels like – glowing embers, heat, and combustion."

"I still can't believe Barbara endangered Zoe's life with that man. On second thought, yes, I can. She abandoned her child for Tariq."

"I still can't believe I'm pregnant."

"You better believe it – you, my baby mama!"

Elijah rests his head against my belly. "Hey, you in there? What's good?" Elijah laughs.

Elijah and Toussaint surprise Zoe and me with a healthy pine tree. The ring of evergreen and spirally leaves bowl like Saint Nick. Brandy gets some therapy, shopping for pale pink, gray, and ivory holiday cheer. Zoe desired pink ballerinas. I fancied an ivory palette, and of course Elijah's preference was gray. Zoe, Mom, Ms. Vela, and I had fun decorating while Elijah was working at "Z" Saturday night. Elijah was pleasantly surprised on Sunday with the progress we made.

"Wow! Babe, the tree looks good."

"Thank you! Zoe wanted to wait for you to put the angel on the top."

"I'm kinda glad it will just be the three of us for the holidays" Elijah mentions.

"Me too!"

Dr. Patterson strongly advised against traveling for the holidays. It didn't matter one way or the other. I was physically in no mood to travel. Elijah and I are content to stay home. Ms. Vela is traveling to Portugal to spend time with her family. Mom usually hosts a small cocktail party on Christmas Eve. This year, I sent my regrets.

"Nikita, I understand. You need time to restore. The trauma you are experiencing both mentally and physically is draining your body. Your body is now operating for two. Get some rest. Everyone will understand. Kiss Zoe for me and hug Elijah. I love you!" Mom responds.

Mrs. Martha was going to travel to Philly for the holidays, but Elijah wanted us to stay low-key.

"Eli, have a wonderful holiday! Be good to yourself and take care of your beautiful family. Eve and I will be in Philly for the custody hearing. Remember, 'Every perfect gift is from above.' Please kiss Zoe and Nikita for me. I love you!"

"Thank you! I love you too, Mom. I hope my bighead sister likes her gift."

"Ha-ha! I'm going to tell her you called her bighead."

On Christmas morning, Zoe and I sleep in late. I wake in prayer, "Happy Birthday Jesus."

"Father God, thank you for blessing the Virgin Mother Mary with a son – our savior, Jesus Christ. Please forgive me for putting my fears before faith. I know I will always be in need of you. Please help me to be faithful to you, Lord. James 1:17 says, 'Whatever is good and perfect comes down to us from God our Father, who created all the lights in the heavens. He never changes or casts a shifting shadow.' Father God, thank you for being the source of my light and my protector. I pray that you cover my family and friends in the blood of Christ. I entrust my health, finances, and career to you. May your power sustain me. May I live in confidence of your provision for me. Thank you for everything you do, including the answers to my prayers and forgiveness of my sins. This confirms in my heart how much you love me. You are a powerful and mighty God. I appreciate your loving kindness, powerful grace, your gracious patience, and mighty heart. May your will be done in me to be a better person, daughter, mother, and friend. All praise to you. "Happy Birthday, Jesus!" Amen."

Elijah put his skills to work making breakfast – fish, grits, and cheese eggs. It is not Ms. Vela's cooking, but the fish is crisp and buttery, the cheese eggs are light and fluffy, and the grits are creamy.

"Merry Christmas, Baby! Something smells good."

"Merry Christmas, Babe! You slept in late. How are you feeling?"

Elijah dishes my plate and pours his coffee.

"My body feels a little tender and sore. I'm surprised Zoe isn't up yet." I note.

"Lay across the sofa. I will set your food up on the tray."

Soon after, we hear little feet running through the hallway.

"It's Christmas! Merry Christmas! Dada, why didn't you wake me up? Where is my KiKi?"

"Merry Christmas, Zoe! I wanted you to get your beauty rest. Nikita is on the sofa. Are you ready for breakfast?"

"Merry Christmas, Zoe!" I exclaim.

"Merry Christmas, KiKi! No, I'm not hungry. Did Santa come?"

"Yes, he did! Go look under the tree." Elijah cheers.

"I will be back to eat. Ooh! Look at the pretty presents. Dada, which one should I open first?"

Elijah hands Zoe two boxes. I sit up on the sofa to watch her open them. She rips the wrapping paper and opens the new doll baby first.

"Oooh! She is pretty! She looks like me when I was a baby. Ha-ha! She has on lip gloss. Her lips are shiny"

"Ok, Zoe! Open the next one." I encourage.

Zoe rips open the box. "It's a shirt."

"What does it say, Zoe?" Elijah asks.

"I am a BIG Sister! Dada, I'm not a big sister."

"You will be, Princess. Nikita is having a baby."

"My Kiki?"

"Yes!"

"A real baby?"

"Yes!"

"A boy or a girl?"

"We don't know yet." I reply.

Zoe jumps up and down. "I'm going to be a big sister. This is the best present ever. When do I get to hold the baby?"

"Zoe, we have six months to go." I respond.

"Where is the baby now?"

"Right here in Nikita's stomach"

"Wow! Can I see?" I lift my shirt. "The baby is in your tummy? How you get it out?"

"The doctors will." Elijah says.

"Aww. You have to go back to the hospital?"

"Yes, but this time you get to visit. You will be visiting your baby brother or sister!" I explain.

"I can't wait to tell Ms. V. I am a big sister."

"Babe, you trading your car in for a minivan?" Elijah laughs.

"No, Baby. I think the car seat and booster will look great in the 'Audi Q7!'"

"Yaasss! In Matador Red!" Ivy shouts.

Zoe happily rejoices and takes well to the surprise. She marvels in anticipation of opening her other presents. Throughout the day, Zoe presses Elijah and me with more questions. "How did the baby get in your tummy? Where is the baby going to sleep? What about your work? Does Auntie Eve and Mom Mom know the baby is in your tummy?"

We lounge lazy all day. Watching some of our favorite Christmas movies – or maybe my favorites: *Almost Christmas, This Christmas, The Preacher's Wife*, and *Friday after Next*. Elijah cooked T-bone steaks, parmesan mash potatoes, and sautéed spinach with garlic and onions for dinner. Ms. Vela left us some holiday cookies. We spread holiday cheer from West Philly to Chicago. Zoe's happiness rose to ecstatic when sharing her news of becoming a big sister.

"Mom, Nikita was worried Zoe wouldn't be happy with the news."

"Eli, Zoe is beyond happy. God is going to reward you for your obedience. Continue to obey what God says and he will watch over you and your family. He saved Nikita and he will take care of Zoe. I am joyful for your season. I am proud of you, Son, and I know your father is too!"

"Thanks Mom. I'm proud of you too. You did a great job raising us!"

"I did – didn't I. With the Lord's help of course. Merry Christmas, Elijah!"

"The devil tried it. This was a joyful and peaceful Christmas. Happy Birthday, Jesus!" Ivy smiles.

CHAPTER 23 –

"Full Custody"

The custody hearing for Zoe is tomorrow. The horrid experiences of the past month are paralleled with the joyful vision of resilience where hope and love reside. Time away from work has helped tremendously in keeping Elijah calm. Yvonne is doing a phenomenal job running the club in his absence. The "Z" community offered up great support in the wake of the shooting. In the five years the "Z" has been open, that was the first incident. Da bruhz are overseeing the real estate projects. Elijah and I have devoted our time and energies to restorative action therapy. The sessions are helping us to examine the nature of our souls.

Zoe gets dressed on her own now. Zoe's pick of the day is a red dress with black polka dots. Zoe has a one-on-one scheduled with the judge. Ms. Vela is also being called as a character witness. Ms. Vela is as nervous as a cat. Mrs. Martha and Mom are going to be right there to hearten her. Those three are Elijah's Angels. I had to love up on Elijah and bring in reinforcements from Eve. Elijah unwillingly agreed to let me accompany him to the custody hearing.

Barbara and her attorney approach Courtroom 1126. In her haste to see Zoe, Barbara bumps into Mrs. Martha.

"Hello, Barbara."

"Hi, Mrs. Martha. I was hoping to talk to Zoe. How is she?"

"When was the last time you talked to your daughter?"

"Elijah has been ignoring my calls."

"Rightfully so. You endangered the lives of my son, my granddaughter, and Nikita."

"I'm so sick of hearing Nikita's name. I am Zoe's mother and I always will be."

"A mother doesn't abandon her child. Barbara, I will pray for you."

The family joins up with each other in front of the courtroom. Eve and Zoe are enjoying hot chocolate with marshmallows in the cafe. Barbara approaches Elijah in the lobby after her encounter with Mrs. Martha.

Barbara lashes out at Elijah, "It is your fault Tariq is in jail. Oh, you mad, Elijah, because Tariq is a gangsta. He is a real man. He takes good care of me."

"Is he taking care of you now? You can't even take care of yourself. I'm not going to let you ruin Zoe's life."

"Elijah, you bastard! You think you have a ready-made family with your bougie bitch. You will not take my child."

"I don't have to. You gave her to me. Remember?"

"Zoe needs her mother. Zoe wants to be with her mother."

"Barbara, we will see what the judge thinks of you as a mother."

Ivy fumes, "That is your antithesis of a real man? This woman is undeniably batshit cray-cray."

CHAPTER 24 –

"Alexander v. Smith"

"**A**ll rise. The court will now hear the case of Alexander v. Smith. The Honorable Judge Latney presiding. Please be seated." The bailiff says.

"**Good morning, Ladies and Gentlemen. Calling the case of Alexander v. Smith. Are both sides ready?**"

"Good morning. Ready for Elijah Alexander, Your Honor."

"Good morning. Ready for Barbara Smith, Your Honor."

"**A petition for primary custody of Zoe Madison Alexander has been filed by Elijah Alexander. The petition for full custody is being contested by Barbara Smith.**"

24.1 – "Ms. Carla Vela"

"**I would like to begin today's proceedings with the testimony of Carla Vela.**"

"Do you affirm to tell the truth, the whole truth, and nothing but the truth under the pains and penalty of perjury?" The bailiff asks.

"I do." Ms. Vela affirms.

"**Good morning, Ms. Vela.**"

"Good morning, Your Honor."

"Ms. Vela, you seem nervous. Relax. I just have a few questions. Ms. Vela, you are employed by Mr. Alexander?"

"Yes. I am Mr. Alexander's house manager."

"Ms. Vela, how long have you worked for Mr. Alexander?"

"I have worked for Mr. Alexander for four years."

"Do you refer to him as Mr. Alexander at work?"

"No, I call him Elijah."

"Tell me about your responsibilities as a house manager."

"I oversee the daily upkeep and maintenance of his loft. I manage the household expenses and budget for utilities, groceries, and HOA fees. I also assist in caring for his daughter Zoe."

"Ms. Vela, how do you assist in caring for Zoe?"

"I prepare meals and prepare her for bed – bath, oral hygiene, and pajamas."

"Do you drive Zoe to and from school?"

"No, Elijah does."

"In what other capacity do you assist in caring for Zoe?"

Ms. Vela laughs, "I am sometimes a guest at Zoe's tea parties."

"Zoe loves tea parties?"

"Yes, Zoe does very much."

"Do you read bedtime stories to Zoe?"

"No, Elijah reads to her at night."

"Have you ever chaperoned a school event?"

"Yes. Ms. Smith said she did not want to go to a smelly zoo so I served as a chaperone in her place."

"Objection, Your Honor. Ms. Vela is speculating." Barbara's attorney objects.

"How do you know she is speculating? Were you there when Ms. Smith declined to chaperone her daughter's trip to the zoo?"

"No, Your Honor."

"Objection overruled counselor."

"Ms. Vela, how would you describe Mr. Alexander's relationship with his daughter Zoe?"

"Zoe is his lifeline. Everything he does is to solidify a positive future for Zoe. Elijah is always present when he is with her. He also enjoys being a guest at her tea parties. Elijah reads her bedtime stories every night. He chaperones school trips. Elijah provides Zoe necessities both basic and beyond. They laugh a lot together and he kisses her boo-boos. Elijah's flexible work schedule affords him the opportunity to stay home with Zoe when she is sick. Zoe is Elijah's princess."

"Ms. Vela, thank you. You may be seated."

"I have a thirty-minute one-on-one scheduled with Zoe Alexander. I will ask you all to be seated promptly at 11:45 a.m."

"Your Honor, Zoe is in the café. May we please have fifteen minutes to bring her upstairs?" Elijah's attorney asks.

"Absolutely. Please have my clerk escort Miss Alexander to my chambers."

"All rise." The bailiff commands.

24.2 – "Miss Zoe Madison Alexander"

"Hello, Miss Alexander. Do you mind if I call you Zoe?"

"I don't mind. My Auntie Eve calls me ZoZo."

"What does your Dada call you?"

"Zoe."

"What does your Mom call you?"

"Zoe. When people are around, ZoZo."

"Who is around when your Mom calls you ZoZo?"

"Mom Mom and Auntie Eve."

"Zoe, do you know why you are here?"

"Yes, so I don't have to leave my Dada."

"Do you like living with your Dada?"

"Yes."

"Do you like living with your Mom?"

"No."

"Why don't you like living at your Mom's house?"

"My Mommy is always mad and there are always clothes in my room."

"Your clothes?"

"No."

"Where are the clothes in your room?"

"On the bed. On the floor."

"Have you seen your Mom lately?"

"No."

"Have you talked to your Mom on the phone lately?"

"No."

"Why do you think you haven't seen or talked to your Mom?"

"She is mad at my Dada."

"Why is she mad at your Dada?"

"Because we had dinner at my KiKi's house."

"Who is KiKi?"

"My KiKi is Dada's queen."

"Who had dinner at KiKi's house?"

"Dada, my KiKi, Mom Mom, Ms. V, Mr. Jesse, and Ms. D."

"You like KiKi?"

"I love my KiKi."

"Do you spend a lot of time with KiKi?"

"Yes. My KiKi helps me with my homework. We go to church. She is having a baby. I'm going to be a big sister."

"Are you excited about being a big sister?"

"Yes. I don't know if it's a boy or a girl."

"Who drives you to school?"

"Dada."

"Who picks you up from school?"

"Dada."

"Who takes you school shopping?"

"Dada."

"Do you read books?"

"Yes. Dada makes funny animal noises when he reads my books."

"Does your Dada go on school trips?"

"Yes. Dada likes skating. Dada likes the lion and tigers at the zoo."

"Zoe, what do you love most about your Dada?"

"Dada makes me and my friends laugh. He kisses my boo-boo. He gives big hugs. Dada says I'm his princess." Zoe giggles, "He always tells me he loves me."

"Zoe, what do you love about your mother?"

"She let me live with Dada."

"I appreciate you talking with me Miss Zoe. Is there anything you want me to know or you want to say?"

"Thank you for helping my Dada."

"All rise." The bailiff commands.

"Please be seated."

"We will recess for forty-five minutes. Please be ready to begin at 1:00 p.m."

24.3 – "Mr. Elijah Alexander"

"All rise." The bailiff commands.

"I hope you all enjoyed your lunch. I know you are all eager to get started. I would like to call to the stand Mr. Elijah Alexander."

"Do you affirm to tell the truth, the whole truth, and nothing but the truth under the pains and penalty of perjury?" The bailiff asks.

"I do." Elijah affirms.

"Mr. Alexander, what do you do for a living?"

"I own and operate a nightclub and lounge in Northern Liberties. I also manage investment properties."

"Mr. Alexander, how many properties do you currently manage?"

"I currently manage five properties."

"Mr. Alexander, do you own these properties?"

"Yes, with an investment group."

"What percentage of each property do you own?"

"I own 25 percent of each property."

"Mr. Alexander, walk me through a typical weekday for you."

"Zoe and I have breakfast in the morning. I drop her to school by 8:30 a.m. I'm in the management office from nine to two. I pick Zoe up from school at 3:00 p.m. We have a snack and talk about her day. We start her homework. My girlfriend, Nikita, helps her with the remainder of her homework. On Thursdays and Fridays, I leave for the club around five. I'm back home by 9:45 p.m."

"Do you work at the lounge on Saturdays?"

"Not as much in the past month. Yvonne is my new general manager. She has been with me for five years. I'm called to work on Saturdays if we have a high-profile event. I will work on a Saturday if a sponsor asks for me to be present. Otherwise, Yvonne is fully capable and has the full support of our team."

"Mr. Alexander tell me about the incident that occurred at your lounge on October 6, 2019."

"Barbara charged into the club, insisting I take Zoe. Barbara claims I was disrespectful when I brought my girlfriend Nikita with me to pick up Zoe. Barbara said she was giving me Zoe to ensure I did not disrespect her or her boyfriend Tariq going forward. I told her the club wasn't a place for Zoe during that hour. I asked her why couldn't I have picked up Zoe during our normal schedule – the next day. Barbara said she and Tariq had a date and her mother was not available to watch Zoe."

"Mr. Alexander, how would you describe your relationship with your daughter Zoe?"

"I'm fun. I discipline Zoe, but she and I talk about her behavior and the consequences for her actions. Although I'm building for Zoe's future, I am always fully present for her. I love listening to her stories. I love to see Zoe's imagination peak when she's playing. I love how Zoe cares about my feelings. I love raising Zoe. I'm a great father."

"Mr. Alexander, thank you. You may be seated. Ladies and Gentlemen, I appreciate your time and patience. We will recess for fifteen minutes."

"I'm glad that's over. I was sweatin' up there."

"Baby, you were truthful. Your delivery was honest."

"Yes, E. It was raw and fueled by real emotion. You are a great father!" Eve acknowledges.

"Eli, Carla took Zoe home."

"We better get back in there." The lawyer insists.

24.4 – "Ms. Barbara Smith"

"All rise." The bailiff commands.

"Thank you. Please be seated. I would like to call to the stand Barbara Smith."

"Do you affirm to tell the truth, the whole truth, and nothing but the truth under the pains and penalty of perjury?" The bailiff asks.

"I do." Barbara affirms.

"Ms. Smith, what do you do for a living?"

"I am a radiology technician."

"How long have you been a radiology technician?"

"Six years."

"Ms. Smith, how would you describe your relationship with your daughter Zoe?"

"I'm her mother. I love her and want what's best for her. I make sure she is happy, has clean clothes, and food to eat."

"Ms. Smith, explain to me what happened during the evening of October 6, 2019?"

"I dropped Zoe off to her father at his nightclub."

"Ms. Smith, did you explain to Mr. Alexander why you brought Zoe to him?"

"Yes, he was disrespectful to me."

"How was Mr. Alexander disrespectful towards you?"

"He showed up to my house with his girlfriend."

"Did Mr. Alexander bring his girlfriend in your house?"

"No."

"Where was his girlfriend?"

"In the car."

"Ms. Smith, who answered the door to your apartment when Mr. Alexander arrived?"

"My boyfriend."

"Ms. Smith, what is your boyfriend's name?"

"Tariq."

"Ms. Smith, who pays the bills in your apartment?"

"I do."

"Ms. Smith, is it true that Mr. Alexander provides you a monthly stipend?"

"Yes, Zoe is his daughter."

"Ms. Smith, what do you use the monthly stipend for?"

"My bills."

"Ms. Smith, is it true you received a shut-off notice for a $900 electric bill and a rent notice for two months of nonpayment?"

"Yes. My mother was sick and I had to help her."

"Ms. Smith, who paid your electric bill and rent during that time?"

"Elijah."

"Ms. Smith, who buys Zoe's school clothes and basic necessities?"

"I put food on the table."

"Ms. Smith, that wasn't my question. Who buys Zoe's school clothes and basic supplies?"

"Elijah."

"Ms. Smith, why did you bring Zoe to Elijah at such a late hour?"

"It wasn't late. It was 6:00 p.m."

"Do you think a lounge is an appropriate place for a small child?"

"Elijah had her birthday party there."

"Ms. Smith, what time was Zoe's birthday party?"

"I don't know. One or two, maybe."

"Ms. Smith, explain to me what happened during the evening of December 7, 2019."

"December 7th?"

"Yes. The night your boyfriend, Tariq Hughes, was arrested."

"Tariq got into an argument with someone at the club. Tariq was defending himself against the bouncer who violated his space."

"Ms. Smith, were you arrested the evening of December 7, 2019?"

"Yes."

"Ms. Smith, why were you arrested?"

"I was trying to protect Tariq from the police."

"Ms. Smith, was Tariq Hughes charged with two counts of reckless endangerment, unlawful possession of a firearm, unlawful discharge, violating probation, and disorderly conduct?"

"Yes."

"Ms. Smith, do you know who Tariq Hughes intended to shoot during the evening of December 7, 2019?"

"No."

"Ms. Smith, did you know Mr. Hughes had a gun in the trunk?"

"No."

"Has Zoe ever rode as a passenger in Mr. Hughes' car?"

"No."

"Whose car did you drive to the lounge in when you brought Zoe to her father?"

"Tariq's"

"I will ask you again. Ms. Smith, has Zoe ever rode as a passenger in Mr. Hughes' car?"

"Yes."

"Ms. Smith, did Mr. Hughes have a gun in the trunk with Zoe in the car?"

"I don't know."

"**Ms. Smith, when was the last time you saw or spoke to your daughter Zoe?**"

"The day I left her with Elijah."

"**Did Mr. Alexander prevent you from seeing or speaking with your daughter Zoe?**"

"Elijah has been ignoring my calls."

"**Ms. Smith, when did you first attempt to contact your daughter?**"

"After I was released from police custody."

"**Ms. Smith, thank you. You may be seated.**"

"**I appreciate your time and attention today. I will review the testimonies provided here today. We will reconvene tomorrow morning at 9:00 a.m. Thank you. Court is adjourned.**"

"All rise." The bailiff commands.

Barbara and her attorney exit the courtroom. She walks out with her head down. Mrs. Martha, Mom, and I leave the courtroom as well. Eve and Elijah stay behind to talk with the attorney. I have three missed calls from Zoe.

"Nikita, how do you feel? I know it must have been painful recalling the night you were shot." Mrs. Martha asks.

"I'm fine. At times, it feels like a dream. Today was a reminder it was real."

"Elijah is a great father. I know the judge can see that. It will all work out." My mom says.

Elijah is quiet the whole ride home. Eve met RiRi at "Z." Eve said she needed a "Happy Hour." We reach the loft and Zoe meets us at the elevator.

"Dada, you're home. KiKi! Mom Mom!"

"Hi, ZoZo, give Mom Mom some sugar!"

"Hi, Zoe!"

"How are you, Princess?" Elijah asks.

"Ms. V made cheeseburgers. Want some?"

"Yes, I am starving." Elijah replies.

"How did it go after Zoe and I left?" Ms. Vela asks.

"We will know tomorrow morning." Mrs. Martha responds. "Nikita and Elijah, you both must be tired. I can look after Zoe if you want to get some rest." Mrs. Martha adds.

"No, I'm good. I'm going to hop in the shower. Y'all eat. Babe, you should get some rest."

"This little one is hungry. I will rest up." I respond.

"I won't be long." Elijah says, kissing my forehead.

Ms. Vela makes the best comfort food.

"Ms. Vela makes the best any kind of food." Ivy notes.

Later in the evening, Mrs. Martha and Elijah talk with Zoe about her one-on-one with Judge Latney.

"Zoe, did you like Judge Latney?" Elijah asks.

"Yes."

"Did you enjoy talking to her?" Mrs. Martha inquires.

"Yes."

"What did you talk about?" Elijah queries.

"She asked me about you and Mommy. I told her Mommy is always mad. I told her I'm a big sister. I told her I love my KiKi."

"Were you nervous?" Elijah asks.

"No. She gave me grapes." Zoe notes.

"Dada, do you have to go back?"

"Yes. Tomorrow."

"And then I can stay forever?"

"I asked God to let you stay forever."

"My KiKi says when you pray, God listens."

24.5 – "The Honorable Judge Latney"

"All rise. The court will continue with the case of Alexander v. Smith. The Honorable Judge Latney presiding. Please be seated." The bailiff says.

"Good morning, Ladies and Gentlemen. This morning I am prepared to render a decision regarding the petition for primary custody of Zoe Madison Alexander. Yesterday, we heard the testimony of Ms. Carla Vela, Mr. Elijah Alexander, and Ms. Barbara Smith. I also had the pleasure of talking with Miss Zoe Madison Alexander. Zoe is a gifted child – happy, curious, kind, and smart. As parents, we try to shield and protect our children from the dangers of the world. Zoe is a precocious child and she is well aware of what is happening around her. Mr. Alexander, you are not a co-parent you are a co-payer. You are co-paying for Ms. Smith's financial responsibilities or lack of responsibility. Ms. Smith, you put your wants before the needs of your child. You endangered the life of your daughter by the company you kept. When someone shows you who they are, trust and believe them. You also abandoned your child. Mr. Alexander did not disrespect you by having his girlfriend wait in the car outside of your apartment. You disrespected Mr. Alexander by having your boyfriend answer the door – the door to a dwelling of which Mr. Alexander pays the bills. It is my decision today to award full custody of Zoe Madison Alexander to her father, Mr. Elijah Alexander. I will schedule a follow-up date to discuss visitation rights. Ms. Smith, since you gave Mr. Alexander your child on October 6, 2019, you will provide child support payments. You will receive further correspondence in the mail for a date to appear in court. At which time, we will review your wage earnings. Thank you for your time and attention. Court is now adjourned."

"All rise." The bailiff commands.

Barbara rises in a fury and flounces out of the courtroom. Da bruhz—Toussaint, Lavon, and Charles—hug it out with Elijah. Mrs. Martha hugs Eve with tears of joy.

"Congratulations, E." Toussaint, Lavon, and Charles bark.

Elijah looks back at me. "I love you." His lips read.

"I love you too! Congratulations!" My lips answer back.

Back at the loft, Zoe is thrilled with the news.

"Dada, I'm glad the judge helped you."

CHAPTER 25 –

"Solomon 8:6–7 NLT"

Elijah and I share bath time tonight with Zoe. I get the bubbles. He gets the flannels. Tonight, story time was a little different.

"You two are the main reasons I smile. Nikita, you don't judge my past and you support my future. As complicated as my life is, you never waver or complain. You are my rib – always by my side. You listen without judgement or conviction. You give me honest talk. We have established a partnership; sharing ideas and building a framework for action. You love my daughter like she is your own. My family, friends, and da bruhz love and adore you. Zoe and I loovvee you. Share our life! Nikita Simone Brown. Marry me! Please! Marry me!"

I feel my eyes grow misty, butterflies in my stomach dance to the melody of my heartbeat.

"Girl, did he just ask you to marry him?" Ivy quips.

"Zoe, what do you think?" I propose.

"You should marry Dada!" Zoe exclaims.

"Listen to the kid." Ivy injects.

"Mr. Elijah! Yes! Yaasss! I will kindly marry you!"

Zoe presents me with a black velvet box. Inside sits a 3-carat square-shaped diamond center stone. The stone is framed with micro pave' diamonds and set on a micro pave' band in platinum.

"1, 2, 3. Green light!" Ivy jokes.

Elijah's kisses catch my tears like joy and excitement capture my spirit. Okay, I am not entirely sure if Elijah bellows a growl, howl, or bark, but his excitement is evident. Zoe's scream indicates she is over the moon.

"Does this diamond ring make me look engaged?" Ivy gushes.

I have been wondering about what my dad and Elijah were mulling over on Thanksgiving. During breakfast, I couldn't dawdle over my tea any longer.

"What were you and my dad laughing about on Thanksgiving?" I ask.

"That's between me and your dad."

"Really? Come on! Give me something!"

"Nope!"

"He gave his blessing? Didn't he?"

"Nikita Simone Brown, I got nuthin' – nuthin' but love for you, baby!"

The next couple of weeks …

"Let's go to Anguilla?" Elijah presents.

"I have to check to see if I can travel."

"Your doctor said it's safe. Marry me in Anguilla! Roo, that belly in a bikini!

"When did you speak to the doctor? Anguilla?"

"When we went to your follow-up appointment. Yes, Anguilla!"

"I got flight and hotel accommodations. You got decorations and catering. You in?"

"I'm in!" I conclude.

The best man, Toussaint, grabbed the reins of an epic bachelor party weekend for Elijah. He took it to the yard – Sin City. Vegas is perfect for a weekend of debauchery – gambling, burlesque shows, cigars, and plenty of Four Roses single barrel bourbon. The guest list of course includes the usual suspects: da bruhz, childhood friends from Chicago, and close associates.

Before the bachelor party moves into a full set, matters of the heart are revealed.

"Touss, thanks bruh for putting this together." Elijah offers.

"Bruh, thank you for showing us every dawg deserves a pussy cat. There is hope in love. Nikita is a good girl. I am happy for the both of you." Toussaint declares.

"Dawg, Nikita's independence, ambition, and strong will doesn't bother you?" Dawuh interjects.

"Dawuh, her independence and ambition inspire me. No doubt, Nikita is stubborn." "She describes it as being determined." Elijah laughs. "She is also fervent and fun. Take her civic engagement for example – the way she supports and educates minority and women-owned businesses. Nikita is the perfect role model for my daughter. Yes, she has her own, but she supports my hustle as well. I love that she shares her strengths and vulnerabilities. I am comfortable in our relationship to do the same. Our relationship is by no means perfect, but we make progress together. That is why I love her and why I asked her to marry me." Elijah assures.

"Dawg, Nikita is alright with me. So is her girl, Nicole." Lavon adds.

"Bruh, Nikita's vibe is amazing. You can't help but feel happy around her." Charles notes.

"Dawuh, it sounds like you only know Nikita's work persona. Elijah and Nikita fit. I have known this bruh a long time. Elijah needed someone to challenge him mentally. Nikita is his sweet spot. Dawuh, you are right. Nikita stands firm in her beliefs. I am enamored by their love for each other. That is my sister and I know she has my back and I have hers." Toussaint affirms.

"Roo, I hope you are right. Smart girls have smart mouths and smart motives. I hope it stays sweet for you." Dawuh protests.

"Dawg, it will! I bet my life on it." Elijah discloses. "Now let's toast to my last days as a bachelor and my sweet life ahead. Be owt!"

Clink! Clink!

"Chocolate" is the star of the evening. Her name matches the richness of her dark cocoa complexion. Chocolate's full breasts embody the globus brown of a coconut. Her ass! Well let me just say, it will shake out a round of applause – it CLAPS! Chocolate will give you a standing ovation! The exotic pleasures of the evening commence. The allure of Chocolate's burlesque show propels da bruhz towards an erotic enlightenment elevated by an expression of Chocolate's sensual happiness. Self-love is a powerful muse. A wicked storm passes quickly around the pole. Da bruhz are causing a rain typhoon for an encore.

On Sunday afternoon, Zoe and I speak with Elijah.

His voice raspy and hoarse, "Hi, Baby girl! How are you doing, Zoe?"

"Hi, Dada! Hope you are having fun! Bye!"

"Hi, Babe!"

"Did Zoe just dismiss me?"

"Yes. She is baking cookies with my mom. You sound like you had fun. Are we still getting married or did you get hitched at the Purple Paradise chapel?"

"Ha-ha! That's hilarious, Babe. We definitely had fun this weekend! I am ready to come home though. I miss you!"

"I miss you too. Did you win any money?"

"I won a couple of dollars at the roulette table."

"Did you make it rain on the dancers?"

"Babe, you know what happens in Vegas, stays in Vegas!"

"Yes, I know. That's probably one of the reasons Touss chose Vegas. He can plead the fifth."

"Exactly! Is your mom going with you in the morning to Zoe's school?"

"Yes, I think so. If not, I will be fine."

"Babe, you are not supposed to be driving."

"I know. I can always use the ride app."

"You know that's not my only concern."

"Elijah, I can't continue to be a hermit. I have to venture outside on my own at some point. I won't push myself if I'm not ready. I will see how I feel tomorrow."

"Please be careful. Tell your mom I said Hi! Ask Zoe to save me some cookies. I love you!"

"I love you too! Get back to your fun, sun, and sins."

Early Monday morning, I use the ride app to take Zoe to school. Mom doesn't agree with my decision to go alone. I can either fall against fear or fly past it. I chose to fly. The sky is a clear blue and the morning air is crisp. Zoe is happy I get to meet her teacher, Mrs. Wilson.

"Good morning, Mrs. Wilson! This is my KiKi!"

"Hi, Mrs. Wilson! I am Nikita Brown. It is a pleasure to meet you. Zoe always talks about you."

"Ms. Brown, I share the same sentiment. How are you and the baby feeling?"

"We are both doing well!"

"I'm glad to see you are doing better!"

"Mrs. Wilson, thank you! I hope you and Zoe have a great day!"

"Zoe, I love you. Have a great day!"

"I love you too! See you later."

I exit the school feeling a bit anxious. A cafe sits on the corner across the street.

"Honey, you can only have decaf." Ivy prompts.

The aroma of the coffee beans stall my anxiety—that is, until I receive a text to my phone. The number I don't recognize, but the men in the photos I do. Immediately, I request a car via the ride app. As the car approaches the loft, I can feel my chest tighten; the space between my lungs is constricting. Sweat beads on my brows. Thankfully, Mom is still at the loft.

"Nikita! Baby, what's wrong? Baby, breathe! That's it – in and out. Sit down. I will get you a cold compress."

"Inhale. Exhale." Ivy whispers.

Mom doesn't chastise me. She doesn't say, I told you so. She just massages my temples and applies the cold compress on my forehead until I fall asleep.

A few hours later, Elijah returns. "Elijah, welcome home!" Mom exclaims.

"Hi, Mrs. D! I am glad to be home. Thank you for taking care of my baby girls. Where is Nikita?"

"Baby, she is sleeping. Your fiancé is mulish like her father."

"What happened?"

"Nikita had a panic attack this morning. She insisted on taking Zoe to school alone. When she got back to the loft, she was in bad shape. That's my daughter and I love her, but she is unyielding when she has her mind set to do something."

"I had a conversation this weekend about how willful Nikita is."

"Elijah, you and Jesse are the only ones who can seem to tame her. Son, good luck."

"How was Zoe?"

"Zoe was great! She listens; Nikita Simone Brown, on the other hand, is stubborn as a mule."

I wake as Elijah enters the bedroom. In my anger and despair, he is still my handsome protector. Elijah sits next to me on the bed.

"Hi." I whisper.

"Hi, Babe! How are you feeling?"

"My mom told you about my panic attack?"

"Yes. What happened?"

"I received a disturbing text this morning."

I pass Elijah my phone and scroll to the text I received this morning. Elijah scrolls through the images. There were fifteen photos in total. Someone wanted to get their point across.

"Nikita, I didn't cross the line this weekend. I wasn't inappropriate with any of these women."

"Elijah, I am not bothered by the photos. I don't doubt your behavior. It was a bachelor party! Let a dawg roam, he will find his way home. Right? What sent me over the edge is someone in your set text me these photos. I don't know this number. Do you? First Barbara, now this. Someone doesn't want us to live our best life."

"Nikita, I will handle this."

Rage dims the light in Elijah's eyes. The taste of salt from my tears covers my top lip. I feel protected by the warmth of his kiss and his arms wrapped around me.

"We will live our best life – together. I am da bruhz keeper."

"First, Barbara bat shit, and now we have stepped in some dawg shit." Ivy yells.

"Get some rest. Don't worry. I will pick up Zoe."

"I'm sorry you had to come home to this."

"I came home to you and Zoe. Nothing else matters. I love you!"

"I love you too!" Elijah exits.

"Mrs. D, Nikita is awake. I'm going to pick up Zoe. Do you need anything while I'm out?"

"No, baby. I'm going to start dinner soon. I will make her and Zoe a snack. Be careful."

Elijah jumps in the Range dialing Toussaint.

"Touss, we got a problem."

"Dawg, what's up? Is everything Roo with Nikita and Zoe?" Toussaint inquires.

"Your bruh sent Nikita photos from the weekend."

"What? Who? Don't tell me that motherfucker, Dawuh."

"Dawg, he is a problem. Imma pay his ass a visit tomorrow."

"You want da bruhz there?"

"No, just me and you. Nikita had a fuckin' panic attack. Knowing what she has been through … and jeopardizing the health of my baby. Bruh."

"Bruh, did he try to push up on Nikita in the past? Is he jealous? What the fuck?"

Tuesday evening, Toussaint and Elijah pull up in front of Dawuh's condo in Brewerytown.

"Touss and E! What y'all doing 'round here?"

"We were in the neighborhood." Elijah answers.

"You gonna invite us in?" Toussaint howls.

"Sure." Dawuh hesitates.

"What happened to how good and pleasant it is when da bruhz dwell in unity?" Elijah demands.

"E, what's up Dawg?" Dawuh probes.

"What the fuck is your fixation with Nikita?" Elijah asks.

"What do you mean?" Dawuh questions.

"I let the shit this summer fade because Nikita handled it herself. But you crossed the line sending her those pics from Vegas. What is your motive? Jealousy? Why the fuck you playing with her emotions? Why the fuck you in my shit? Were you hoping for a shot with Nikita?" Elijah howls.

"It wasn't like that." Dawuh replies.

"What was it like? Help us to understand. We don't covet da bruhz life. We are a collective—we build, not tear down." Toussaint injects.

"I crossed the line. At work, Nikita thrived off of chaos and change. A part of me wanted to know if she embodied that same resilience in her personal life. I was looking out for you."

"Looking out for me bringing chaos and confusion into my life?" Elijah yells. "Stay the fuck out of my affairs. Nikita is not a fuckin' case study. The next time it won't be a conversation. The next time we'll take it to the yard. If you are my bruh, respect your pledge. Our friendship is essential to the soul. Loyalty is all we have."

"Roo, bruh. Like I said in Vegas, Nikita is my sister and I got her back. That was fowl, Dawg." Toussaint adds.

"I will apologize to Nikita." Dawuh offers.

"No! Leave Nikita the fuck alone! Deal with your own head space." Elijah scoffs.

Back at the loft, Elijah seems preoccupied.

"Elijah, is everything okay?" I ask.

"Babe, I'm good. Touss and I had a problem to work through. Everything is fine now."

Elijah grabs my waist and kisses my belly.

"How are you and the baby feeling? Hey you, in there!"

"We are doing much better today." I reply.

"In a couple of weeks, you are going to be my wife. I won't let anything or anyone jeopardize that. I got you babe."

"I know. I got you too."

"He handled the problem. I know it was that fuckin' askhole, Dawuh." Ivy scoffs.

Before going to bed, I pray over Solomon 8:6–7.

"Place me like a seal over your heart, like a seal on your arm.

For love is as strong as death, its jealousy as enduring as the grave.

Love flashes like fire, the brightest kind of flame.

Many waters cannot quench love, nor can rivers drown it.

If a man tried to buy love with all his wealth, his offer would be utterly scorned."

CHAPTER 26 –

"Eternal to the Soul"

Swaying in a hammock outside our beach villa, the peaceful blue umbrella above covers Zoe and me in the warmth and tranquility of Anguilla. Aqua waves appear on the sand when the sun soaks into the ocean. Our beach villa overlooks the Caribbean Sea and the mountains of St. Martin. The manicured landscape is a lush green with swaying palms. The breeze is a welcome guest to the sun baked sand underfoot. The organic vegetables tender augmented by the succulent and ripe garden fruit. Karee is our cabana boy – cute handsome with a bright smile and dimples. Virgin Strawberry Daiquiris happily delight our soft palate. The movement and kicks from my belly suggest a little someone likes them too.

Before we left Philly, my girls planned an intimate bridal/baby shower brunch. The theme was Winnie-the-Pooh and Tigger too. I'm a huge fan of Hundred Acre Wood – also simply known as "The Wood." I love the innocence of Pooh and the energy Tigger possesses. I have bouncy fun reading about Pooh's adventures. Yvonne designed a specialty Mimosa cocktail infused with ginger and agave honey. Too bad mine didn't have alcohol in it. Nudged by the Vegas debacle, I wanted something intimate and sweet.

"April bridal showers bring May wedding flowers." Ivy smiles.

On the dawn of the ninth day of May, Matthew 19:6 evokes my consciousness: "So they are no longer two, but one. Therefore what God has joined together, let man not separate."

White gives freshness and grace to the look of the wedding party. Zoe frolics around the bridal villa in a beautiful white dress with chiffon butterflies. Elijah and da bruhz clean up handsomely in white tailored linen suits. My dress is white chiffon with a bateau neck bodice, balloon sleeves, and a plunging V back. The seamstress left room for my baby bump and ass plump. My crown is adorned with vibrant, luscious blue hydrangeas, baby breath, and ivy. Centered in the palm of our hands, the bridal bouquets are of the same arrangement. The fullness and sweet dewy aroma of the bouquets fly blissfully through the breeze. My girls are downright gorgeous sheathed in linen. Eve is sexy and strapless. RiRi looks saucy in her halter. Joie's crisscross vibe is so coquettish. Nicole's neckline produces a sweet sensibility against Brandy's sensual straps.

The vanilla cake with buttercream icing is simple yet elegant. The cake is tiers of blue and white rosettes. The topper reads "Mr. & Mrs. A." The weather is a perfect 80 degrees for a beach side ceremony. The whisper of the breeze by the aquamarine water is a calm cascade of cool. Elijah flew in DJ Mackey from Germantown for entertainment.

Last night, Mom, Mrs. Martha, and Ms. Vela had one too many daiquiris at the rehearsal dinner. I'm glad my girls are here because "Elijah's Angels" are hung way over. I guess since I couldn't drink, they lushed up for it. Thank goodness they remembered something borrowed and something new. I have something blue covered. Mrs. Martha lent me her mother's blue sapphire earrings. The earrings were a gift from Mrs. Martha's father in celebration of her parents' 45th wedding anniversary. Mom surprised me with a new ankle bracelet charmed with an elephant.

Dad knocks on the door of the bridal villa. "KiKi, Baby. They are ready for you."

"Aww. Look at my baby girl. You look beautiful!"

"We do look beautiful, barefoot, and pregnant." Ivy compliments.

"Thank you, Dad! Are you ready for this?"

"Are you ready for this?" Dad smiles.

"Absolutely! I prayed for this!"

"I must say, KiKi. You got a good one."

"Thank you, Dad!"

I chose Beyonce's, "Dangerously in Love" instead of the traditional bridal chorus. As RiRi would say, that's our song. Zoe sprinkles petals from blue and ivory hydrangeas along the sand. The sand warms my feet. The flow of the dress against my bare feet and the sand tickles. As Dad and I proceed down the sand, I can feel the rhythm of his heartbeat in his hand. I lay my head on his shoulder to let him know I will always be his baby girl. Elijah looks handsomely delicious. His waves are on spin. He is fidgeting with his boutonnière. Mom, Mrs. Martha, and Ms. Vela are already shedding tears.

"Welcome, family and friends! We are gathered here today to bear witness and celebrate the marriage of Nikita and Elijah. This is a testament of God's glory and grace. This union is the answer to their prayers.

Nikita and Elijah have spent precious time getting to know each other, and we now bear witness to what their relationship has become. Today, they will affirm this bond formally and publicly on the beautiful sands of Anguilla. This affirmation of their love means more because it is shared with their loving family and friends.

Who gives this woman to marry this man?"

Tears rolling down his face, "I do." Dad declares.

"Today, Nikita and Elijah will mark their union and love for each other. They celebrate the love of their daughter, parents, siblings, extended family, and best friends. Love is universal.

Nikita and Elijah, today you not only marry one of God's children, you also commit to being a servant of the Lord.

Each of you have written your own Vows."

"Nikita!"

"Elijah, I prayed for you. I prayed for us. My day begins and ends with the thought of you. Your eyes light my soul. Your smile warms my heart. My heart and soul are filled with you. We have faced the warmth of the sun and the cast of dark clouds. Still, God's promise held true. I promise to be honest and faithful. I promise to be supportive and patient. I promise to be kind and humble. Elijah, I thank the Lord for you."

"Elijah!"

"Nikita, your smile won my heart the first time I laid eyes on you. Your kindness, your grace, your beauty, and your strength are why I fell in love with you. You have been my right hand and never complained or wavered. You made me believe in love again. You made me believe in me. I will cherish, love, and protect you and our family always. Nikita, I thank the Lord for you."

"Do you Nikita take Elijah to be your lawfully wedded husband? To have and to hold, in sickness and in health, in good times and not-so-good times, for richer or poorer, keeping yourself unto him for as long as you both shall live?"

"I do!"

"Do you Elijah take Nikita to be your lawfully wedded wife? To have and to hold, in sickness and in health, in good times and not-so-good times, for richer or poorer, keeping yourself unto her for as long as you both shall live?"

"I do!"

"A ring is an unbroken circle, with ends that have been joined together. It represents your union. It is a symbol of your infinite love. When you look at these rings on your hands, be reminded of this moment, your commitment, and the love you share for each other."

"Elijah, place the ring on Nikita's finger and repeat after me."

"Nikita, I give you this ring as a symbol of my love with the pledge to love you today, tomorrow, always, and forever."

"Nikita, place the ring on Elijah's finger and repeat after me."

"Elijah, I give you this ring as a symbol of my love with the pledge to love you today, tomorrow, always, and forever."

Elijah and I hold hands.

"Nikita and Elijah, before these witnesses, you have pledged to be united in marriage. You have now sealed this pledge with your wedding rings."

"By the authority vested in me by The American Marriage Ministries and the British Overseas Territory of Anguilla, I now pronounce you husband and wife."

"Elijah, you may kiss your bride!"

Elijah wipes away my tears and leans in with a kiss. I feel a flutter and a kick. I place Elijah's hand on my belly.

"You feel that?"

We both smile and kiss like no one is watching.

"We's married now." Ivy yells.

The beach is our backdrop for the wedding portraits. The photographer flicks first with the full bridal party, then the parents. Elijah and I pose for serious and silly photos with Zoe. The girls and I sashay and slay our photo shoot. Da bruhz Greek hand-signs gestures in their photos. Elijah and I have fun taking our photos while everyone enjoys the hors d'oeuvres and cocktails. After our pictures, DJ Mackey gets a signal to ask everyone to stand.

"Family and friends, may I please ask you all to rise? With great pleasure, I would like to take this opportunity to introduce Mr. & Mrs. Elijah Alexander."

We chose Michelle Williams' "Say Yes" as our entrance song. It's Caribbean flava mixes in joy and love.

Karee and the wait staff serve a delectable main course of grilled chicken and pineapples, jerk shrimp, rice pilaf, and grilled mixed vegetables. In a loving display, we make our way around the tent with hugs and kisses for everyone. Zoe is on the dance floor with Dad. We suggested some playlist options for DJ Mackey with hits for hours. We selected songs to bop, step, slide, whine, and twerk to. Dad and I dance to Chrisette Michele's *Your Joy.*

Elijah and Mrs. Martha glide across the dance floor to Teddy Pendergrass' *"You Are My Latest, Greatest Inspiration."* Elijah and I step in Chicago fashion to Marvin Gaye's *"Come Get To This."* Eve and Elijah step it up to *"Jazzy Lady."* Later in the program, Elijah and da bruhz surprise us with a step show.

"We are the brothers of Q Psi Phi,

The Mother Pearl and that's no lie,

We're gonna live, we're gonna die

In the name of Q Psi Phi"

The step show frenzy works up the bridal party. The baby kicks every time Elijah barks, "Woof."

"Babe, the decorations are nice. I'm surprised you chose blue. Your favorite color is teal." Elijah mentions.

"Well, I guess now is as good a time as any."

"What do ya mean?"

"Now is a good time for one of your wedding gifts."

"A gift? Marrying me was a gift."

"Elijah, I chose blue because pink wasn't an option."

"You don't like pink." Elijah points out.

"I chose blue as a surprise!"

"Surprise. What surprise?"

"Elijah, we are having a boy!"

"Wait! What? A BOY! No bullshit?"

"Yes, Babe. We are having a BOY!"

"Surprise!"

"Facts? A BOY!"

"Yes, Elijah! A BOY!"

"Nikita! Baby! Thank you! A son!"

"Mr. & Mrs. Alexander, what's happening over here? What are you two up to?" Eve asks.

"Something borrowed. Something blue. The blue is a boy!" Elijah exclaims.

"What boy?" Eve jokes.

"We are having a BOY! The baby is a BOY!"

Now everyone is wondering what is happening. I was going to save the news until the toasts.

"E, what's up bruh?" Toussaint asks.

"A son! Nikita is having a boy!" Elijah screams.

"Dawg, Congratulations! I want to be like you when I grow up. Congratulations, E!"

Elijah asks DJ Mackey for the use of his microphone.

"Can I have your attention everyone?" Elijah asks.

He can barely speak. Zoe and I stand in front of the stage.

"Karee, please make sure everyone has a glass in their hand." Elijah insists.

"I'm sorry to take everyone off the dance floor. I have some news to share. Today is one of the best days of my life. I married this beautiful woman and everyone we genuinely, truly love is here. I didn't think this day could get any better – but it did. Nikita didn't share any details of the wedding planning. I was okay with whatever she chose. Everything is wonderful – the food, the music, the decorations. Right! The blue is a nice touch. My thought was the blue signified something blue. Right! I'm about to blow your mind. In a good way. Please everyone, raise your glasses. I would like to toast to "Something Blue" is also "Something New." Nikita and I are having a BOY! We're having a BOY!"

"Yay! A little brother! Yay!" Zoe shouts.

Zoe and I hug and toast with Pineapple Juice.

"Bruh! Congratulations!"

"This is wonderful news!"

"Aww! What a great surprise!"

"A grandson!"

"This is great news!"

"I'm so happy for you both!"

"That is a clever surprise!"

"ZoZo, you're going to have a little brother!"

"Roo!"

"Congratulations, KiKi!"

Congratulatory hugs and kisses are coming from all sides. I have to pat myself on the back – not bad Nikita. This was a great surprise.

"Something blue is something new! That's cute." Ivy giggles.

"Well, since we already have a glass in hand, as the Best Man I would like to share a few words. E and I have known each other since college. Elijah has always been a good bruh. The kind of bruh there when you need him and there when you think you don't. Elijah is a great father and a great friend. Nikita, I know he will be a great husband. Elijah always has these ideas and plans. By the time he comes to you with it, he has already done the research and worked out the numbers. Elijah has the strategy, model, and rate of return figured out. I trust him. I trust him with my money. I trust him with my future. I trust him with my life. Elijah, we are da bruhz. I love you, Dawg. Our friendship is eternal to the soul. Omega Psi Phi until the day we die. Be owt!" Toussaint toasts.

"Roo!" Lavon and Charles howl.

"It's my turn." Joie yells. "As Zoe says, my KiKi is my good, good girl-friend. Nikita doesn't let anything stand in her way. Nikita is a force – her spirit is soaring. She is classy and caring. Nikita is intelligent – a girlboss for sure. Nikita can also be a lion if you push her. Watch out, Elijah. That lion roars—loud. But most importantly, Nikita is a beautiful queen. Nikita, I wish you and Elijah the best. May the Lord continue to bless you and keep you in his favor. I love you both."

"Ok. Make way for the big girl - belly coming through. It's my turn. Thank you all for the love and support you have given Elijah, Zoe, and me. You have all been with Elijah and me from the beginning – through the sun, rain, and rainbows. I pray you all will continue this magnificent journey with us. I appreciate you all traveling here to Anguilla. This has been a special day and I thank you for sharing it with us. Elijah, I love you with all that I am. Zoe, thank you for making me a better person. To my parents, thank you for your unconditional love. I pray I am to my child what you have been for me. To my girls, Joie, Brandy Nicole, and RiRi, thank you for always adjusting my crown. To my little man, I can't wait to meet you. God bless each and every one of you. Thank you!"

DJ Mackey takes his cue and starts the real party in Lil' Kim form. Ain't no party like a "Queen Bee" party.

I've always had high self-esteem, but baby! Pregnancy makes your skin glow, your hair shine, and your boobs big – like real big. Sexy is as sexy does. Tonight, my wedding night, I feel like the Queen of Sheba. Elijah is feelin' nice. He drank enough for both of us. My boobs and belly pop in a light-blue open front, silk nightgown with lace trim.

"Mrs. Alexander, blue is now one of my favorite colors – after purple of course." Elijah says.

"I'm glad you like it, Mr. Alexander."

Elijah turns on the music to Ushers' *"Hard II Love"* discography. We dance in one rhythm in the moonlight on the balcony of the villa. Elijah's sapid fragrance rests under my nose. I can feel the hairs stand on his arms and neck from the cool air off the water.

"I love you, Mrs. Alexander."

"I love you too, Mr. Alexander."

Elijah's tender kiss is gentle. His touch is careful and soothing. His caress is soft yet lingering. Elijah lifts and carries me to the bed. Elijah's lips outline my neck and breasts. His lips brush my belly with slow, feathered kisses. Elijah's forehead rests on my belly, his hands rest on my sides. Elijah's muscular torso rises. He spreads and enters between my legs with relaxed and steady strokes.

"Are you comfortable?" He asks.

"Yes." I moan.

His thrust is gentle and slow. His breathing is calm. I squeeze his hands and he squeezes back. My pussy covers his penis in wet secretion. I tighten my pelvic muscles alongside his strokes. Each Kegel drizzles secretion from my pussy – coating his scrotum. His penis lies wet cloaked in the warmth of my pussy. My grip on his penis draws his climax near. Elijah pushes heavier strokes with his pelvis. A squishing sound plays off of each stroke. The melody drives Elijah crazy. He squeezes my hand hard. Elijah's climax matches my orgasmic peak. He exhales and slides down to lay his head against my belly. My fingers trace the spin of his waves.

"Whoever said pregnancy sex is the best sex – ain't never lied." Ivy moans.

CHAPTER 27 –

"Highest Point"

I haven't been sleeping well for a couple of weeks. There is no comfortable sleep position the baby agrees with. If I lay on the right, he kicks. If I lay on the left, he kicks. He just wants to get out. Dr. Patterson recommended a C-section to deliver the baby. She is concerned about the shock my body experienced last year. June 15th is the day we welcome our new little prince.

I've exhausted the nesting phase decorating our new home. We were sold on the charm of East Mount Airy. The charm is captured on display in the beauty of bright floral filled boxes and majestic natural landscapes. The mature trees provide welcome shade on the wrap around porch. Zoe and I had to have a porch swing. The character of the home spoke to the needs of our growing family. Elijah's real estate company manages my house as a rental. Elijah also kept the loft and leased it to the real estate company. It now serves as da bruhz new office space.

Elijah let me loose into my element. I love home décor. In an effort to pair my bohemian style with Elijah's modern industrial, we compromised on a Middle Eastern design aesthetic. The walls are veiled in Morocco Sand. The parlor is flanked by two Indonesian wood daybeds covered in rust velvet. The living room is accented by brass side tables and wood carved cabinets. A nearby console is ornamented with sculptural lamps, ceramic pottery, energy crystals, and books in our reading rotation. Texture was added with silk and linen Ikat pillows set upon wool floor coverings.

Ms. Vela lives in an in-law suite in the basement. The parlor houses the sitting, dining, and family rooms. The kitchen is nestled between the dining and family rooms. The deck outside the family room is a peaceful haven for coffee and prayer in the morning. Nature's surround is a great office alternative on a sun-soaked day. Ms. Vela sources herbs, vegetables, and fruits right from the backyard garden she planted. The guest and children's rooms occupy the second floor, along with their playroom. Our offices are tucked away in the attic. The third floor plays host to the master bedroom suite and an additional guest bedroom. Although its current use is as a man cave. Zoe's room is an enchanted forest layered in chartreuse and pink. I fanned after the "Harlem Toile" wallpaper in the hall bathroom of the loft. We chose that same wallpaper by Sheila Bridges in green for a wall panel in Zoe's room. The vibe in our home is light and airy, a relaxed atmosphere. People kick their shoes off and lounge. I always catch somebody in a private meditation. It may also be the cocktails – Yvonne is still queen of a cocktail.

The hospital bag is packed and sitting by the door. Mom is staying at the house with Ms. Vela to care for Zoe. Elijah's plans for paternity leave are supported in partnership with Lavon who will increase his responsibilities at the management company. Yvonne and her team are fully equipped with resources to manage "Z."

The morning of the C-section, Elijah and I have breakfast in the garden. This may be the last peaceful moment we have before the baby arrives.

"Whatever happens today, I need you to know that I love you very much. I am proud of you and eternally grateful for your support." I confess.

"Nikita, I know. You're scaring me. This C-section is safe? Right?" Elijah replies.

"Yes, but life happens. I don't want to ever miss an opportunity to say, I love you, thank you, or I'm sorry."

"I get it. My mom says, 'Our time and season are connected to our obedience.' I love you too. My boo-boo 'bout to have my baby."

Zoe runs out to join us in the garden.

"Ms. D said I can come to the hospital to see my little brother." Zoe says.

"Yes! Are you excited about being a big sister?" Elijah asks.

"Yes! Can he sleep in my room?"

"Not yet, Zoe. He has to sleep in our room for a little bit." I answer.

Mom and Ms. Vela gather for coffee.

"Nikita, are you ready?" Ms. Vela asks.

"I'm equally anxious and nervous. I can't wait to meet our little prince."

"Well, you two better get going. Your life is about to change in a blessed way. Your father and I are happy for you both." Mom praises.

"We are blessed – blessed with an amazing village." Elijah declares.

The admissions staff verifies my insurance coverage and emergency contact information. Elijah has been on the phone with his mom and Eve all morning. Although Elijah has been through childbirth before, his anxiety is on 100.

"Elijah, are you sure you want to witness this? One of the girls can switch places with you."

"No. Nikita, I got this."

"You sure?"

"God's got this. He's got us!" Elijah exclaims.

"Mrs. Alexander, you are going to feel a pinch. You may experience some discomfort. Ready?"

"Ready! Elijah, you ready?"

"Yup! I'm ready, Babe. I love you."

"I love you!"

Forty-five minutes later, Elijah and I welcome Zion Miles Alexander. Zion weighs in at seven pounds and eleven ounces. His stretch is long from the top of his full black hair to his tiny toes. Now I know why I always had heartburn. We matched Zoe's initials, ZMA. The meaning of Zoe is life. In

Genesis 3:20, Adam called the name of his wife, Zoe, for she was mother of all the living. Eve came to be from Adam's rib. Elijah named Zoe in homage to his sister, Eve. Zion signifies the Kingdom of Heaven. We chose Miles as his middle name in remembrance of Elijah's father, Miles Alexander.

Faintly, I can hear the voices of the doctor and nurses. My body is trembling against my cold extremities. Elijah's voice is pleasantly near.

"Nikita, he has ten little fingers and ten little toes. He is beautiful. Babe, thank you!"

There is nothing sexier than a man who puts his pride aside. A brief but beautiful moment seeing Elijah vulnerable – tears of joy and thankful prayers for his new blessing.

"Father God, thank you for being the source of my light and love. My mother always prays over James 1:17, 'Whatever is good and perfect comes down to us from God our Father, who created all the lights in the heavens. He never changes or casts a shifting shadow.' Thank you for being patient with me. Thank you for testing me. Thank you for Nikita, the answer to my prayers. She breathes life into me. She breathed life into my son. Thank you for my beautiful family. Amen."

The next day, Zion and I welcome the family at the hospital.

"Nikita, he is precious." Mom cries.

"E, man you did it! A new generation of Omega Psi Phi." Charles says.

"His fingers are tiny." Zoe giggles.

A few weeks ago, Elijah and I asked Joie and Toussaint to serve as godparents. They were both humbled by our request. We were honored when they said Yes.

Back at the house, we have all settled into our new normal. I sleep when Zion sleeps. Elijah's sleep schedule is crazy. He jumps up for every gasp, burp, or twitch. Elijah is always rocked during Zion's feeding schedule. His night feedings are at midnight, 2:00 a.m., and 6:00 a.m. Ironically, those are the times I would take bathroom breaks while I was pregnant. Zion is a drunken sailor after eating. One night, Elijah was done with me. After I showered, we had a brief but intimate moment. Funny enough, Elijah did. He became intimate with my breast milk or as Nicole calls it, liquid gold. Zion started crying, my breasts leaked, and squirted Elijah in the eye. He was not happy or aroused after that.

My parents pitch in with Zoe for grandparents weekend. She ditches us for my mother's choco chip cookies and Disney movies. My parents love spoiling Zoe and Zion.

"Zoe, are you excited about your sleepover with my parents?"

"Yes. I'm glad Zi is not going. He cries too much." Zoe says.

"Zoe. I know it seems like he cries a lot. That's how he tells us what he needs. He cries for a diaper change. He cries when he's hungry. He cries when he is cold or hot." I explain.

"I like Zi when he's smiling."

"Zion loves you. He always smiles when he sees you."

"I love my brother too – I just don't like when he cries."

"Zoe, can you please save me some cookies?"

As the indigo sky dances with the stars, my thoughts runneth over. Brown has Elijah crowned. I simmered a Hot Toddy spiked with bourbon, ginger peach tea, raw honey, and lemon. I extended a heavy hand to the bourbon. Hopefully, Elijah and Zion will sleep through the night. Zion is smiling at the angels. "Now I lay me down to sleep. I pray to the Lord my soul to keep ..." As I gaze at my king and my little prince sleeping, feelings of peace, innocence, love, and light holy my spirit.

CHAPTER 28 –

"Mwen Fini"

Post pregnancy is a full experience. My breasts are full. My hips are full. My locs are full. I am full – I am full and I am in love …

I am in love with being a mother. I am in love with being a wife. I am in love with being a servant. I am in love with being God's child. I am in love with myself.

"Gurlll, please don't stop breastfeeding. I am in love with these new breasts." Ivy boasts.

Girl prays morning, noon, and night.

Girl goes to a premier nightclub.

Girl sleeps with the nightclub owner.

Girl dates the nightclub owner.

Girl falls in love with the nightclub owner.

Girl gets shot at the nightclub.

Girl marries the nightclub owner.

Girl grows her family with the nightclub owner.

"Regrets? Nope! I love me some Black Licorice!"

"Hey, Mrs. Alexander!" Ivy closes.

The END!

EPILOGUE

They say that passion dies within a marriage. They say that external factors within a marriage create chaos. They say that communication within a marriage lies mute. Who are they? Are they married? Now that Elijah and I are married, I am happily committed and compelled to please him, listen, understand, and support him more. I never want him to forget any of the reasons he chose me as his wife.

I've built a home in my heart for my husband. Our relationship is not perfect. Sometimes there are storms in our veins. But blessings flow in abundance through our blood.

He understands and appreciates my independence and my vulnerability. We continue to build our relationship mentally, physically, and financially. Our foundation is set upon consistency, compromise, and empathy.

Oh my! Last and certainly not least ... he satisfies my sweet tooth. He is tall, dark, salacious, sweet, and spicy! Yaaasss – like a piece of black licorice!

KIKI'S PRAYER

"**F**ather God, my heart and love belong to you. Thank you for your blessings over my life. Thank you for your blessings over my heart. I offer you this meek heart of mine.

Father God, thank you for your blessings over his heart – whoever, wherever he may be. I pray he fears you. I pray he adores you. I pray he loves you. I pray he is humble. I pray he is patient. I pray he is kind. I pray he is loving. I pray he is honest. I pray he is ambitious. I pray he has a sense of humor. I pray he is obedient to your will. I pray his heart is full of passion and discernment. I pray he is sensitive and vulnerable to the Holy Spirit.

Father God, please guard his heart and cover his soul in your Grace. Cover him in the blood of Jesus Christ so he may seek you in times of joy, happiness, pain, and despair.

Father God, please let us be happy in silence. Let us be present for each other in the spirit of the Lord. Let us be happy when the bills arrive. Let us be happy when we agree to disagree. Let us be happy in the company of family and friends. Let us be happy when it rains and pours. Let us be happy when the sun shines and the breeze blows. Let us listen to understand and not listen to respond. Let us cry in the Holy Spirit and laugh with the Holy Spirit.

Father God, please protect me in the midst of danger. Comfort me in my afflictions. Strengthen my temporal needs. Heal my body of pain and discomfort.

Father God, please bless this union so that we may live in you and for you.

Father God, I thank you for all that I am and all I will continue to be. I pray I follow your plan and purpose.

Father God, I claim your powerful and victorious favor over me. In the Lord's name I pray.

Amen."

ACKNOWLEDGEMENTS

"It always seems impossible until it's done." **Nelson Mandela**

F irst and foremost, thank you to my Lord and Savior for your unconditional love and blessings.

Thank you to my inner voice *"Ivy"* for your playfulness, adventure, curiosity, creative and feisty spirit.

Thank you to my son, Charles *"Toussaint"*, for your sense of humor, love,
and patience. Thank you to my parents, Karen *"Delores"* and Eugene *"Jesse"*
for instilling in me confidence, care, and love. Thank you to my sisters, Jontue
"Joie" and Myisha *"Nicole"*, for being Dope Girls who always support and
check a sista'. Thank you to my Day 1s, Roxanne *"Rochelle"*, for always being in
perfect harmony, and Brandilynn *"Brandy"*, for always being a cutie patootie.
You are my favorite #BrunchBabes. Thank you to my aunts, Camille *"Elaine"*
and Jacqueline *"Yvonne"*, for your unwavering love and support. Thank you to
my brother, Noel *"Lavon"*, my brother-in-law, *"Charles"* Randy, and #CheDad,
Hans *"Mirko"*, for being phenomenal fathers. Your presence and guidance
are invaluable in weaving the fabric of our future leaders. Thank you to my
nieces, nephews, and cousins: Damir, Darien, Devan, Maki, Miles, Nair, Nia,
Xavier, and Zion. You each have a unique talent and ability to always create
and cultivate #blackgirlmagic and #blackboyjoy. Thank you to my sister-in-
law, Traci *"DJ Tra"* for always spinning your support my way. Thank you to
my spiritual mother, Ms. Val *"Latney,"* for posturing me in faith and prayer.

DP, thank you for inspiring me and my love of storytelling. You will
always be at the center of my heart. Thank you to my sista', Lynette *"Raw*

Dawg", for teaching me how to be a big girl. Thank you to my god sisters, Gerbie*"Patterson,"* Robin *"RiRi"*, and *"Llona"* Shelly, for your laughter, libations, and listening ears. Thank you to my god brothers, Ceez and Paul, for your grit and entrepreneurial hustle.

Thank you to my focus group, Trevin ΩΨΦ, Tara, Tiffaney, Michelle, Cydney, and Anita for sharing your time, candor, and enthusiasm. Thank you to my design team, Garfield Dawkins, Jhade Gales Designs, Primelens Photography, Joie Candle Co., and Najee Poles for capturing my vision and sharing your outstanding artistic talents.

Philly! Philly! Thank you for raising a jawn. Thank you for your gift - street smarts, resilience, and love. Hollywood & Vine (62), my soul is eternal to you!

Where Brooklyn @. I am forever grateful to Brooklyn, NY, for teaching me the dream is free and the hustle is sold separately. The culture of grit and grind is ever present in the souls of Brooklynites. Thank you to my Boston squad, #TeamNNF, for your civic engagement, leadership and #PettySquad antics.

Lastly, I want to thank YOU – the reader for taking this journey with me through my imagination, art, and design.

Peace, Love & Licorice!

Camille Creates

FOOTNOTES

1. **Brunch Babes**, noun, A group of good, good girlfriends who enjoy bottomless Mimosas, French Toast, and Gossip.

2. **brnd.n3w**, noun, Casual clothing of style worn especially by members who don't follow trends but inspire them.

3. **Quitch**, noun, A "Queen Bitch" who has the tendency to display a resting bitch face and/or behavior.

4. **Jawn**, noun, (Philly dialect) used to refer to a thing, place, person, or event that one need not or cannot give a specific name to.

5. **Roo**, exclamation/noun, Used by da bruhz to give an affirmative response – Yes! Yeah! That's Right! Thank you! Good job! Ok!

6. **The Divine 9**, noun, The National Pan-Hellenic Council (NPHC) is a collaborative umbrella organization composed of historically African American Greek letter fraternities and sororities. The nine NPHC organizations are collectively referred to as the "Divine Nine."

7. **Askhole**, noun, An annoying person who always seeks your input and never takes action or executes the plan.

8. **Son ya (you)**, verb, To demean or disrespect.

BRAND APPAREL
REFERENCES

Chapter 1, 18

Clothing Brand: brnd.n3w

Creator: @doseofdevan

Artistic Director: Devan Nicole

Website: brndn3w.com

Chapter 3

Clothing Brand: Kimberly Goldson

Artistic Directors: Kimberly Goldson and Shelly Powell

Website: kimberlygoldson.com

Chapter 5

Feet Art Brand: The Sneaker Galerie

Brand Ambassador: @na.boog

Director of Sourcing: Nair Pettigrew

Social Network: @thesneakergalerie

Chapter 1, 3, 9

Sneaker Brand: Adidas

Sneaker Model: The Superstar (1969)

Nickname: shelltoe

Website: adidas.com/superstar

Sneaker Brand: Adidas

Sneaker Model: Stan Smith (1965)

Website: adidas.com/stansmith

GENERAL REFERENCES

Chapter 25

The Book of the Bible: Song of Solomon

Bible Verse: 8:6–7

Bible Translation: New Living Translation

Chapter 26

Organization: Omega Psi Phi Fraternity, Inc.

Founder(s): Frank Coleman, Edgar Coleman, Oscar J. Cooper, and Dr. Ernest Everett Just

Founded: November 17, 1911 (Howard University)

Historical Tribute: The Mother Pearl